Also by Bryon Williams

The Grumpy Old Withered of Oz

The Twilight Escort Agency

Code Name Millicent:
The Cat Intelligence Agent Who Came Out of the Cold

Tourist from the Light

The Reluctant Psychic

Naked Warrior

A Light at the End

The Psychic Spy

Not in the Public Interest

The Burning Boy

Shrine of Vengeance

by
Bryon Williams

The Burning Boy

Copyright BRYON WILLIAMS 2020

ISBN – 978-0-6484238-7-4

Email: Bryonwilliams044@gmail.com

Subject: Crime – thriller – action adventure

Copyright Cover Design – Bryon Williams and Emma Gloede

Dedication

For my son Ben and all the other sons and daughters whom I pray will never again be forced to take up arms to defend their freedom.

Introduction

The sun was just beginning to set behind the distant mountains, casting a reddish golden glow and purple shadows over the valleys of the surrounding countryside. There was a sense of quiet stillness and uninterrupted peace.

Two elderly men stood silently, heads bowed, deep in thought before the concrete effigy of an unknown soldier. The inscription on the plinth read, *'In memory of the brave men and women who paid the ultimate sacrifice for their country in the line of duty.'*

Beneath, the record of previous conflicts was inscribed, *'Vietnam War – 1962-1980.'* And below the line, *'At the going down of the sun, and in the morning, we shall remember them,'* someone had roughly painted a line of black graffiti on the ancient, weatherbeaten memorial: ***'And all those who survived.'***

The younger of the two men, a slightly balding, plump little Vietnamese man with a kindly face, placed his hand on the arm of his Australian friend and whispered, 'It's time to go, Steve.'

Steve, despite the onset of old age, still retained the essence of the now-faded qualities of the strong, attractive young man he once had been. He shook himself from his reverie, nodded and turned. Walking with a slight limp and aided by a cane, he slowly made his way back towards their car.

'Y'know, Tan,' Steve said, 'I think this will be my last time.'

Tan patted his old friend's shoulder as he opened the passenger door and smiled.

'What's the matter, you poor old bastard, not feeling too well? Getting ready for the Pearly Gates, are we?'

Steve bristled as he bent to climb into the passenger seat. 'I can still give you a whipping, you bloody old power point.'

Tan chuckled as he pushed the door closed, moved around to the driver's side and slid behind the wheel.

'No, I've got to let go, Tan,' Steve continued seriously. 'This will definitely be the last time.'

'You said that last year, Steve, and the year before that, and ...'

'Alright, alright,' Steve interrupted testily, 'don't go all oriental on me, just drive.'

On the way home to Port Melbourne, Steve sat silently, hardly noticing the familiar passing scenery. Although he had now determined it was finally time to bury the past, he turned his head and looked across at his old friend and business partner who sat hunched over the wheel, concentrating on the road.

'Why do you keep coming back, Tan?'

Tan paused and then shrugged in his typical oriental way.

'Respect ... Atonement.'

In his mind's eye, Steve again saw the handsome, charismatic Vietnamese youth who had saved his life and as is the way of older people, he could not stop his mind wandering back to the distant past when they were young and to the events that had almost destroyed them both.

Chapter 1

It was October 12, 1980, and in the sterile, clinical gymnasium, Steve puffed and strained as he pedalled an exercise bike. Electrodes, cables, headphones and sensors were attached to him, originating from a bank of monitors and dials nearby.

He was now almost thirty, tall, with an impressive muscular build, short, dark, curly hair with early signs of grey beginning to appear. From his determined expression and dark blue eyes it was difficult to read his mood or what he was thinking or feeling; his face was a mask of utter concentration.

Before him was a screen exploding with graphic scenes of war: a horrific audiovisual montage of gruesome sights and amplified sounds of battle: explosions, flames, vicious hand-to-hand combat, bloodied, wounded men, fighting, screaming in agony. Dying. But only an occasional twitch of his eyes and laboured breathing betrayed any reaction.

Intercut with the horror were sudden scenes of sublime peacefulness; soft, misty mountains, calm oceans with dolphins playing, open deserts and rolling landscapes, children running and laughing along a golden beach: quiet, gentle scenes.

Steve's face barely reflected the changes in the scenes before him. His eyes remained resolute but his breathing was heavy with beads of sweat gathering into tributaries that flowed down his straining, glistening arm, chest and neck muscles, soaking into his pale grey tracksuit, spreading into dark patches of perspiration stains.

He was undergoing what his therapist had devised as an 'emotional flooding process'; the theory being if the mind was regularly flooded with disturbing images and contrasted with pleasant images, it would eventually become desensitised to the disturbing images and able to accept the contrasts more readily, thereby causing them to lose, lessen or level out any emotional impact. It was part of a fairly new and experimental treatment designed for returned Vietnam veterans who were suffering from Post Trauma Stress Syndrome, as it was then described. In the first two world wars it was known as 'shell shock' or 'battle fatigue' and mostly unsuccessfully treated with drugs, rest and recuperation. Many never fully recovered.

Not that Steve was actually a returned soldier. He had been a young, contracted news cameraman but his eagerness to record the real experience of combat took him close to the front line of the action many times and he had witnessed horrors he had never imagined possible: the horrors that man was capable of committing against his fellow man. His mind had eventually paid the price.

Dr Robert Heston PhD, experimenting and specialising in Neurological Rehabilitation, stood watching the gauges and dials and taking notes of the readings. He was in his early thirties, from a wealthy background, traditionally good looking, tall, well built, with straight blonde hair expensively fashioned in the style of the seventies. A white technician's lab coat covered his dark grey Giotto suit.

Heston's particular interest lay in the fairly new study of Post Trauma Stress and it occupied his thinking almost to the exclusion of anything else. His manner was professional, but clinical and lacking any real warmth. He switched off the projector and amplifier.

'Alright, Steve, that's enough for today. A half-hour session on the punching bag and that should do you. Then wind down, have your shower and get changed. I'll see you in the office.'

He walked to Steve and began disconnecting the leads. Steve slowed his pedalling, allowing his system to cool down and unwind.

'Well, Doc, how did I do today?'

'Not bad, not bad at all,' Heston replied absently while studying the chart.

4

When the doctor had left, Steve fiercely pounded the punching bag that was plastered with hand-written signs that read, 'Fear!' 'Injustice!' 'Murderers!' 'War!' and the like, with powerful blows that caused him to sweat even more profusely. After the allocated time, he stopped punching but his breathing rate remained high for a couple of minutes until he purposely controlled it with deep intercostal diaphragmatic breathing and steadfastly brought it back to normal.

The steaming hot shower helped to blast the tension from Steve's body. His reflection in the shower room mirror showed heavy scarring on his back, left shoulder, rump and leg. Turning off the water, he grabbed a nearby towel and began briskly rubbing himself down. He dressed in a pair of light grey slacks, a white short-sleeved cotton shirt and slip-on shoes, stuffed his discarded track suit into his sports bag and, with a slight limp, made his way to Heston's office.

He knocked and entered to find Heston sitting behind his desk, writing up his notes on the session.

Steve smiled and said, 'So, Doc, how am I feeling?'

Heston looked up and returned the smile. 'You tell me.'

'Never better.'

'Well, I'd go along with that diagnosis,' Heston agreed.

Steve allowed himself an even bigger smile. 'It's good to have a second opinion.'

He sat in the chair opposite Heston, who referred to Steve's file.

'Pretty constant reaction readings over the last five weeks … Not bad.'

'Does that mean I'm out of the woods?'

Heston shrugged, not prepared to commit himself. 'Let's say it looks promising … very promising. How are things going generally? Any depression or anxiety attacks?'

Steve got up, moved to the window and looked out at the early spring Melbourne morning. The mist had lifted with the promise of a fine, warm day.

'Nothing major.'

'Headaches?'

Steve shook his head.

'Temper explosions? Aggression?'

Another negative response.

'Any trouble concentrating or remembering things?'

There was a pause while Steve turned to look at him blankly.

'What? Sorry, did you say something?'

Heston smiled and Steve laughed at his own gag.

'What about the nightmares?'

The smile disappeared from Steve's face.

'Occasionally; not as often as before.'

'Not a big problem?' Heston asked.

Another pause and Steve replied, 'Nothing I can't handle.'

'Enough pills?'

Steve nodded as Heston wrote final notes on the file.

'Good. Well, I'd say most of it's in your hands now. But keep up your group therapy sessions. Barring any catastrophe, you should go from strength to strength.' Heston smiled professionally without it quite appearing too warm and said, 'I'd say you're on your way home, mate.'

Steve grinned back, hardly able to contain his elation.

'You still want me back next week?'

Heston considered for a moment. 'Let's leave it for a month, see how you go. But if you have any doubts, any problems, call me.'

Steve stood and shook Heston's hand vigorously and gratefully. 'Thanks, Doc.'

As Steve walked to the door, Heston asked, 'How's Sally?'

Another grin as Steve turned and replied, 'Wonderful. You know, Doc, I don't want to downgrade your treatment but if it hadn't been for Sally I think the answers to those questions you just asked me might've been a lot different. It's funny but when I first met her at that party of yours, I thought she was the original Ice Lady, way out of my class. And when she started showing a bit of interest I thought she might have been slumming – you know, out for a bit of rough trade on the side just for a giggle.

Well, you know how I was then, Doc; I couldn't have followed through even if I'd wanted to.' He paused thoughtfully. 'But now …' the boyish grin again, 'it's just wonderful. She's a very special lady.'

Heston made another note and allowed himself an almost imperceptible nod of satisfaction as Steve left the office.

Chapter 2

The SS *Luger*, an old, disreputable-looking, rust-streaked cargo ship, ploughed its way through the international waters of the Southern Indian Ocean. It was travelling just outside what was then the twelve-mile limit of the Australian continent, which could now be vaguely seen on the dazzling, blue, sunlit horizon. On board, the crew went about their business but along the port-side rails, a row of rather poorly dressed passengers pointed and chattered excitedly as they gazed out towards the distant landfall. Their Asian faces betrayed their nervousness, anticipation and relief, tinged with fear of the unknown.

Towards the end of the line, an elderly Vietnamese couple, Nguyen Diem and his very frail-seeming wife, Cuc, stood quietly, not joining in with the excitement. There were tears in Diem's eyes. His wife noticed them and squeezed his hand. Embarrassed at being caught showing his emotion, he quickly wiped the tears away with the sleeve of his well-worn jacket.

She merely smiled and reassuringly stroked his arm.

'Our son will be so surprised to see us.'

On the bridge, Captain Jonas looked out to sea through his binoculars while the ship's mate, Ben Brandwell stood beside him, watching the refugees with a cynical smile.

'Look at 'em,' he sneered. 'They can smell it ... almost taste it.'

But Captain Jonas was watching something up forward. He handed Brandwell the binoculars. 'We've got company.'

Brandwell took the glasses and followed Jonas' directions. In the distance, what appeared to be a Royal Australian Navy River Class launch was approaching. Jonas moved to the ship's tannoy microphone, flicked the switch and announced, 'Now hear this.

8

This is Captain Jonas speaking. A Royal Australian Navy patrol boat is approaching off the port side. There is no need to panic. We are still in international waters and they have no jurisdiction. They'll probably take a look at us and pass on by. All passengers will move back away from the rails until they pass. If they do request to board, keep calm and return below. I repeat, there is no need to panic.'

Having Jonas' words translated by several of the refugees in the queue, his instruction not to panic of course was completely ignored and the refugees began to scatter away from the railings, chattering even louder in fear. At that moment a crew member arrived on the bridge with a radio message. He handed it to Jonas who quickly read it, looked up at the crewman and nodded. 'Confirm. Permission granted.' The crewman retreated from the bridge as Jonas and Brandwell shared a conspiratorial look.

With a protective arm around his wife's shoulders as they moved well back from the rail, Diem whispered, 'We must not worry. The captain assured us that their organisation would look after us. We have their guarantee.'

But his wife was not quite as gullible. 'Many of our people have been tricked with false promises.'

To which he replied, 'We have paid them a great deal of money. And they appeared quite eager for us to join the group. I am sure they will honour their contract.'

He sounded more confident than he really was, trying to reassure his wife's concern.

'Besides, if things come to the worst, we will appeal to the Australian Government. You are ill. You need treatment.'

Cuc looked at him sadly and gently reminded him, 'They refused us before.'

Diem tried not to show his fear and patted her arm. 'We were not this close.'

Gently he took her by the arm and led her off to where the patrol boat was beginning to come alongside. She was very weak and needed his support.

The skipper of the patrol boat, Captain Bryce, a rugged, middle-aged naval type, accompanied by a couple of uniformed crewmen, boarded, making their way up the ladder and arriving on deck just as Captain Jonas and Brandwell joined them.

Jonas' manner was friendly and relaxed while Bryce appeared cordial, but stern and official, and the inscrutable Brandwell stood nearby watching with cold, hard eyes.

Jonas stepped up to Bryce, extending his hand and smiling warmly.

'Welcome aboard. I'm Captain Jonas and this is my mate, Mr Brandwell.'

The ship's mate nodded.

Bryce introduced himself. 'Captain Bryce, Royal Australian Navy.'

'This is an unexpected pleasure, Captain,' Jonas smiled. 'I mean, we are still in international waters, so how can I help you?'

Bryce looked around, taking particular note of an obvious group of bedraggled refugees whose curiosity had kept them on the deck.

'Yes, you are still in international waters, Captain – just.'

He walked over to take a closer look at the decidedly uncomfortable group of refugees and turned back to Jonas with a smirk.

'Part of your crew, Captain?'

'Yes,' replied Jonas, attempting to smile disarmingly.

Bryce studied the group carefully and they became very quiet and tense under his gaze.

'Mixed lot,' Bryce said as his casual scrutiny fell on Diem and Cuc. 'And who would these two be, the cabin boy and the laundry lady?'

Jonas shrugged and gave an amused grin. 'You gotta take what you can get these days.'

Bryce wandered back to confront Jonas. 'And no doubt they've all got their appropriate papers?'

Jonas smiled, again he hoped disarmingly. 'Well, that could be a bit of a problem.'

Jonas led Bryce to one side but their conversation could still be overheard. Diem translated quietly for the other refugees as Jonas continued in a reasonable tone to Bryce.

'Captain, these people are genuine refugees and as such …'

But Bryce interrupted him. 'Wrong, Captain, the Australian Immigration Department decides if they are *genuine* refugees, not you – or me.'

He turned to the group and addressed them, raising his voice a little, making sure he would be heard and understood.

'If you intend entering Australian waters, you will be boarded by members of the Immigration Department who will process your papers. If you fail the Department's medical examination, or if you are suspected of having criminal connections of any kind, or you can't convince the Department that you would be in personal danger if you return to your country of origin,' he shook his head hopelessly, 'you haven't got a hope in hell of getting in.'

'What would happen to us?' Diem called out.

Bryce shrugged. 'I don't really care. As long as you don't try to land on Australian soil.'

'We were actually planning to sail on to New Zealand,' Jonas quickly interceded. 'Their refugee laws are a bit more tolerant.'

Bryce smiled cynically, 'You think so?'

The refugees began to noisily babble their objections but Bryce ignored them and turned abruptly to Jonas.

'Now, Captain, I'd like you to make a space available for me to carry out preliminary interviews with these people.'

Jonas nodded reluctantly and turned to Brandwell. 'Mr Brandwell, have the passengers line up outside the mess.'

Brandwell returned the nod and signalling a couple of crewmen standing by, moved towards the refugees who continued jabbering in protest, as Jonas escorted Bryce back along the deck. When they were out of earshot, out of the corner of his mouth Bryce said, 'How'd I go?'

Jonas gave a nasty smirk. 'Scared 'em shitless – as usual.'

*

Sally Grimes entered the rather dilapidated old building that housed the Brunswick Migrant Advisory Service and made her way down the corridor to her office. She was a remarkably attractive girl in her late twenties, slim, rather tall with short, dark hair, tinted auburn, and blue eyes that at first gave the impression of a very serious, business-like lady but could suddenly change to reveal the playfulness and humour beneath with people she knew and liked.

Dressed in a smart, tailored, navy blue suit with a white, ruffle-necked shirt underneath, she walked purposefully towards her office, nodding and greeting a few of the migrants she recognised sitting and waiting in the corridor. She opened the door leading to the reception desk, entered, and warmly acknowledged Glynnis, the receptionist.

'Hi, I'm back.'

'So I see,' replied the pretty, plump, older woman. 'How'd it go?'

Heading towards her office, Sally turned and pulled a face. 'It was all a misunderstanding. The manager apologised and said he was *appalled* the girl thought he was harassing her. He explained the factory is very small and he was just *easing* his way past her.'

With a cynical look Glynnis replied. 'Easing? With a hard-on? Seventeen times a day? What'd you say?'

'I told him if it happened again I'd *ease* past him and *ease* his scrotum over his head.'

Glynnis giggled. 'You didn't.'

12

'Well, maybe not in so many words but I think he got the idea.'

Sally disappeared into her office, went to her desk, opened her handbag, touched up her makeup and checked her hair in her compact mirror. She put her handbag on top of the filing cabinet, turned to her business diary and opened it but before she could continue with her work, the office door opened and Mr Wey, a well-dressed, middle-aged Chinese businessman, poked his head around the door.

'And how is my favourite social worker this morning?' he said with a broad, warm smile which always made Sally think of a Buddha. 'Winning the battle against ethnic oppression?'

Sally returned the smile, obviously pleased to see him.

'Not entirely, I'm afraid, but we have our little victories. How are you, Mr Wey?'

'You have a minute, Ms Grimes?'

Sally smiled and stood, pointing to her visitor's chair. 'For you, anytime.'

'Thank you,' he said, easing himself onto the chair. 'I thought you would be interested to know that I have taken care of Chen Wing and his family.'

Sally was thrilled. 'That's marvellous! How did you manage it?'

Mr Wey shrugged dismissively. 'It does not matter. The only thing that is important is that they will not have to move out of their home now.'

'And who's picking up the tab – again?' Sally smiled.

He shrugged again, self-deprecatingly. 'I know how hard it is moving to a strange country. I have done well. It is my duty to pay for my good fortune.'

'Well, you're certainly doing that, Mr Wey.'

Changing the subject, he produced a manila folder from his briefcase and pushed it across the desk to her.

'Now, with regard to the Asian Orientation picnic: there are a couple of points I would like to discuss with you.'

Chapter 3

Jonas and Bryce entered the captain's cabin. Both men were relaxed and had dropped their official manner. Bryce removed his cap, tossed it on the bunk, and sat in a chair. 'How was the trip?'

'Not bad,' Jonas replied, moving to a cupboard and removing a bottle of Scotch and two glasses which he placed on his desk and began to pour. 'Bit of excitement one night off the Cocos Islands – fucking band of pirates.'

'Any damage?' Bryce asked.

Jonas shrugged. 'One of the crew was sliced up a bit, woman passenger was raped. Brandwell shot the randy little bastard. Nothing serious.'

Bryce chuckled as Jonas handed him his Scotch.

'What you'd call a killer of a climax, eh?'

Jonas smiled.

'We'd doubled the watch as usual but a few slipped through but we got most of 'em before they could get over the rail. One of the boys lobbed a stick of gellie into their junk. Seemed to discourage 'em.'

'Would tend to,' Bryce smiled and sipped his Scotch. 'Well, anything interesting in this batch?'

Jonas shrugged and returned to his desk picking up his drink.

'Pretty much the same as usual; too long on a waiting list – or not a hope in Hades of qualifying.'

He sat at his desk, removed a folder from the drawer and continued as he skimmed through the contents.

'A few Viets who made a packet out of graft during the war and had to get out of the country to spend it, a Khmer Rouge killer who got a bit over enthusiastic and blew away his section leader, a dope runner from Thailand …'

'Well, he'll come in handy,' Bryce chuckled.

'No doubt that was the company's idea,' replied Jonas as he handed the folder to Bryce.

'What about the old couple? Isn't it a bit unusual transporting nogs that age.'

'They're a special case. He speaks fluent English … and, he's a chemist.'

Bryce nodded his understanding.

'Useful. What's wrong with the old lady?'

'What d'you mean?' Jonas said, looking up sharply.

'She looks like she's gonna cark it any minute.'

Jonas really hadn't noticed.

'She's just old. We'd only get him if she was allowed to tag along. Surprised she's lasted the distance.'

'It's more than age, mate,' Bryce replied knowingly.

Jonas made a mental note to check this out.

'I got instructions through Bangkok that they were to be included.'

Bryce drained the last of his drink and stood. 'I'll see what I can pick up when I talk to 'em.'

'What's the word on the Coastal Protection mob?' Jonas asked as he downed the last of his drink and joined Bryce at the door.

'What there is of them,' he replied caustically. 'The Naval patrol boats are miles away to the south on exercises. An RAAF coast patrol flew over at first light this morning heading east. They would've reported your position.'

'Well, that's no problem. Our course is confirmed to Auckland with a cargo of farming equipment as far as the Port Authorities are concerned.'

'Well then, you're pretty clear.'

'Good,' said Jonas. 'We can do without company for the next few hours.'

*

A light hearted Steve exited Heston's building and paused to enjoy the sensation of happiness and relief at being momentarily cleared by his therapist. As he started to walk down the street he passed a flower stall. He stopped, returned to the stall and purchased a large bunch of purple and white lysianthus to take home to Sally.

*

The last few refugees were lined up outside the door of the mess waiting to be interviewed, their faces strained and tense. Some of them were holding whispered conversations. Brandwell and a couple of the crew stood leaning against the bulkhead, watching. Suddenly the mess door was flung open and one of the refugees stormed out muttering curses under his breath. Brandwell and the other crew members straightened and tensed, ready for any trouble. The refugee glared at Brandwell and turned to the others, speaking heatedly in broken English.

'Hopeless! It is hopeless! None of us will be allowed in!'

Furiously he stepped towards Brandwell who eyed him coldly.

'This is why we came to you!' the Asian man bellowed. 'We have been made fools of! There is no risk, you told us! We were promised safe entry into Australia! Papers, documents, and even work if we wanted it! We paid for it! We paid a lot for it!'

Bryce's voice was heard from inside the mess, 'Next.'

Nervously the next man entered the mess but the disgruntled refugee was not finished yet.

'If we are sent back, word will spread! No one will fall into your trap again! Your organisation will be finished! You hear me?' he screamed.

Suddenly, and violently, Brandwell erupted into action. He slammed two successive punches hard into the man's stomach. The Vietnamese gasped, doubled up and crashed to the deck. A couple of the other refugees moved to protect and assist their comrade but Brandwell was too quick for them. He whipped out a .22 calibre hand-gun and covered them, which forced the would-be defenders back against the bulkhead while the other two crewmen stepped in threateningly. The refugees cowered back in fear, leaving their comrade writhing on the deck at Brandwell's feet.

Chapter 4

A battered old five-tonne truck kangaroo-hopped its way along a country road on the outskirts of Melbourne. It was making terrible grinding noises as it limped along the road emitting clouds of stinking black exhaust fumes. The driver, a wiry Aussie character named Ken Splicer, was in an absolute rage of frustration, cursing the machine as if it were a capricious girlfriend.

'Come on, *come on*, Su-Su you evil bitch! I should've known you'd pull a swifty on me,' he yelled as he ground the clutch into another gear. 'Come on, you bloody slack whore, the first fuckin' decent country-haulin' job in three months an' you have to go and get ya fuckin' period!'

He thumped his calloused fist on the dashboard and continued the tirade.

'Well, tough luck baby, 'cause you're goin', see?'

He slammed his foot on the clutch and again attempted to change gears but Su-Su was not having any of it.

'Shit!' he screamed in frustration.

He stuck his hand out of the driver's window and beat the side panel of the door in his anger.

'Get your arse into gear! Come on. Come *ON*, Su-Su, my little baby,' he pleaded, changing tack and almost cooing. The clutch crunched into gear and Su-Su jumped forward.

'Good girl, my sweet-arsed little darlin'.' Splicer smiled displaying a row of yellowing teeth surrounded by his sun-wrinkled face.

A frustrated car driver roared past blasting his horn.

'Fuck off!' Splicer yelled after the fast-receding sedan.

Su-Su continued to whine, shudder and complain as she lumbered down into the outskirts of the city and into the suburbs.

Heading for Elwood and Steve's garage, Splicer was pulled over by a police patrol car, their blaring siren warning him off the road.

'Oh, fuck!' he sighed, as he pulled over and leaned out of the driver's window.

He pleaded with the two patrolmen saying that he only had to go another couple of blocks to his mate's garage and then everything would be fine.

He was ordered to follow them to the nearest police station and produce his road-worthy certificate or they threatened to confiscate the truck.

Unashamedly playing the poor, hard-done-by Vietnam vet, who was trying desperately to make a living and support a moaning non-existent wife and five kids, they eventually relented and allowed him to proceed on his way with a stern warning and a ticket requesting him to produce the road-worthy certificate within twenty-four hours. Any further discussion was curtailed by a radio message requesting their attendance at an accident back along the highway.

Eventually, with much cajoling, cursing and swearing that would have made a hooker blush, he was able to encourage Su-Su to give her all and finally arrived at Steve's garage, where she came to a shuddering stop outside the service bay. Splicer exploded from the driver's cabin and on the verge of apoplexy, immediately began to thump Su-Su's hood and bonnet and kick her panels and tyres, as he continued to berate her.

'You slimy shit!' (Kick) 'I oughta drive you straight into the fuckin' Yarra!' (Kick) 'How'd ya like that, doll face?' (Thump) 'Muddy water up ya exhaust an' rust in ya carburettor!' (Thump)

He stormed around to the front of the truck and glared straight into her radiator. 'Got scared, didn't ya? You thought if I did this job I might make enough dough to trade you in? Didn't ya? ... Well, you were bloody right! I'll get that nice, clean, reliable Merc we saw last week. Hah! How'd ya' like that, ya' rusty slut?'

But there was little response from the seriously exhausted vehicle apart from a loud, leaking hiss of air from a rear tyre, which sounded for all the world like a resounding fart of protest.

The young, slim, attractive Tan, now in his early twenties, alerted by the abuse and commotion, appeared out of the workshop and stood, hands on hips, grinning at the not unfamiliar sight of Splicer berating and physically attacking the love of his life. Wiping his hands on an oily rag from his pocket he meandered over to Splicer and asked, reasonably, 'Woman trouble again, Splicer?'

'Don't talk about it, Tan, don't talk,' he grumbled. 'Steve around?'

'No, he's out for a while. What's up?'

'What's it look like? Bloody Su-Su's come down with malaria. She's shakin' like a fuckin' AK47 with hiccups.'

Tan smiled at this not infrequent behaviour of Splicer's.

'I'd say she seems to be running a bit of a temperature.'

'You fuckin' amaze me,' Splicer replied drily. 'Can you have a look at her?'

Tan glanced back into the workshop and grimaced. 'Tomorrow?'

'Aw, come on, Tan, I've gotta present a road-worthy to the cops in twenty-four hours and I've got a haulin' contract out in the country. They'll fuckin' cancel me.'

'I've already got an urgent job on the hoist, Ken.'

'I'll give ya a hand to put her up on the manual hoist –Come on, mate,' he cajoled.

Tan rubbed his hand over his jaw, trying to decide if he could somehow accommodate Splicer's predicament, and finally relented.

'Okay, we'll have a look at her but I can't promise anything.'

Splicer heaved a relieved sigh and made his way over to Su-Su.

'Right, this is ya last chance, ya cantankerous bitch. Either shape up or it's el cruncho over the nearest fuckin' cliff.'

He climbed in the cabin and fruitlessly attempted to get Su-Su's engine started just as Steve drove into the yard and parked near where Tan was standing. Reaching for the bunch of flowers he'd bought, he got out of the car.

'You been raiding the cemetery again?' Tan observed dryly. 'You'd better give them to the captain of your support group,' he said, nodding towards Splicer. 'He needs a roadworthy and he's got a hauling contract out in the country and Su-Su just died on him.'

'Typical,' Steve replied, grinning.

After a pause and trying to sound unconcerned as they made their way to Splicer and Su-Su, Tan asked, 'And how did you go today?'

Steve replied casually, 'Not bad.'

He looked at Tan who was obviously desperate for more details, laughed good-naturedly and relented.

'I don't have to go back for a month, unless I feel I need to.'

Tan grinned broadly and playfully slapped Steve on the back. Steve laughed again and ruffled Tan's short, black hair and they began to mock-wrestle like two happy young kids playing in the schoolyard. Eventually Steve draped his arm over Tan's shoulders and they wandered off towards Su-Su and the irate Splicer.

*

Back in the *Luger's* mess, Captain Bryce sat behind a table interviewing a swarthy, shifty-eyed Asian man in his early forties going under the name of Hoang, which in all likelihood was a false name. Hoang was forced to stand facing his seated interrogator to increase Bryce's dominance over the nervous refugee. Diem sat nearby at the table acting as an interpreter. Hoang looked at Diem suspiciously wondering if the old man was a collaborator or a secret part of the organisation. Bryce added to the tension by making Hoang wait while he finished reading a file which lay open on the table in front of him.

He glanced up, noticing the suspicious look Hoang was giving Diem.

'Mr Diem is acting as an interpreter.'

'I do not need an interpreter,' Hoang shot back. 'I would speak with you alone.'

Bryce silently appraised the man and then nodded to Diem, who rose and left the room. Bryce calmly returned to appraising the file.

'No passport and no identity papers, I see.'

'I told you my village was flattened to the ground. Everything was destroyed.'

'Oh, what a shame,' Bryce smirked sarcastically, 'Surely you've had time to replace them?'

'I did not dare apply. I was on the NLF's wanted list. I escaped to Cambodia.'

Bryce glanced at the file and calmly added, 'And then into Thailand where you worked for a dope-running syndicate out of the Golden Triangle. I see you had a little problem with your section head – you blew his head off. You were eventually picked up in a government raid and imprisoned in Bangkok. With outside help and considerable bribery you escaped in 1974.'

Hoang's eyes widened, stunned by the detail of the file on him.

Bryce looked up, laughed harshly, and continued.

'With that record, do you think you'd stand a chance of getting into Australia, or any other country if it comes to that?'

There was a long pause while Hoang slyly re-evaluated his position. Eventually, and not surprisingly to Bryce, the wily refugee played his trump card.

'I have gold,' he whispered, his eyes narrowing conspiratorially.

There was another pause while Bryce appraised him.

'How much?'

Hoang opened his shirt revealing a money-belt around his waist. He opened one of the bulging pockets and removed a small ingot which he placed on the table in front of Bryce. Bryce leaned forward to pick it up but the refugee quickly covered it with his hand.

'There would be more … once I am safely ashore.'

Bryce leaned back in his chair and smiled.

'Lucky you didn't fall overboard. With that lot, you would've gone straight to the bottom.'

There was another pause while Bryce appeared to be considering the proposition. Then he said, 'I'll see what I can do.'

Hoang removed his hand from the nugget and Bryce leaned forward and picked it up.

Meanwhile, Brandwell was still standing over the fallen refugee who huddled on the deck clutching his stomach and groaning. Captain Jonas walked down the ship's corridor and calmly took in the scene.

'Trouble, Mr Brandwell?'

'Not really,' he replied.

'Get him back to his bunk.'

Brandwell replaced his gun, roughly pulled the man to his feet and dragged him off down the corridor. Jonas turned his attention to Diem, standing apart from the rest at the end of the line.

'Where's your wife, Mr Diem?'

'She is not feeling well,' he replied evasively. 'I will answer all of the questions for both of us.'

'What's wrong with her?'

Diem tried to cover up his wife's condition.

'She is old and tired. The strain has been too much for her. She will be better after she has rested.'

'I hear she hasn't been well for a while now?'

Diem smiled nervously.

'No, the long trip, and now this,' he raised his hands helplessly, 'has weakened her … She will be well soon.'

'Just the same, I think you'd better take her down to the infirmary.'

That in itself was a joke as the infirmary consisted of a grubby cabin with a couple of rusty steel bunks, a table with a bulkhead and door separating it from the other areas of the hold which held the equally filthy hammocks.

Diem became even more nervous but still maintained his impassive Vietnamese smile.

'I'm sure that will not be necessary.'

Jonas's face hardened. 'I think it is. I'll send Mr Brandwell down to give you a hand.'

'But, Captain …'

Jonas' look stopped him from continuing.

'It's not a request, Mr Diem.'

Having made his point, Jonas walked off down the corridor.

Chapter 5

Steve's car pulled to the kerb outside the Brunswick Migrant Services building just as Sally was exiting through the front door onto the street. When he honked the horn to attract her attention and waved, she stopped and waved back. He jumped from the car and ran to her holding out the bunch of flowers he'd bought.

'Hiya, gorgeous. How'd you like to make love right here on the pavement?'

Sally laughed. 'You've been watching too many commercials. Besides, it'll cost you more than a bunch of flowers.' She paused, smiling at him. 'I take it your visit with Robert went well?'

Steve could barely control his excitement.

'Couldn't be better. I'm off the hook for a month's trial period ... on the condition I have sex at least twice a day,' he added smoothly.

Sally gave a mock groan.

'Oh, well, if that's what the doctor orders,' she looked at the flowers, 'you'd better get a job at the flower market.'

He kissed her quickly and suddenly remembered.

'Oh, by the way, I'll be home a bit late. I'm having a drink with the guys after work.'

Sally smirked. 'So much for doctor's orders.'

'Hey, they're part of my support group,' he retaliated innocently.

He kissed her again, turned to go back to his car, changed his mind and came back to kiss her again.

'I'll ring Interflora.'

She laughed as she watched him jump back into his car and pull out into the traffic.

'Then why was your application denied?'

Bryce was sitting opposite Diem who, with head lowered, was tentatively trying to answer Bryce's questions.

'My wife failed the medical examination,' he answered quietly.

Bryce studied the old man carefully. 'TB?'

Diem nodded reluctantly. 'We are both very old. Even with successful treatment it could be years before we could re-apply. We thought we would never see our son again.'

This was a bit of information the organisation *didn't* have. He raised his eyebrows and asked, 'You have a son in Australia?'

'Yes, he is the only one still alive. We lost four children in the war. Their school was bombed by the Americans. A mistake, they said.'

Bryce smirked. 'Friendly fire.'

'But not so friendly,' Diem replied.

'And where does your son live?'

'In Melbourne. He doesn't know we are coming. So you see, he would look after us. He would see that his mother received proper treatment.'

'Is he an illegal too?'

'Oh, no, he was sponsored. He is now a citizen,' Diem replied proudly.

Bryce made a few notes on his pad. 'What's the boy's name and where does he live?'

Diem suddenly realised that he may be putting his son in grave danger and refused to answer. But Bryce persisted.

'We need proof that your son does actually exist.'

But Diem had dealt with officials before. He took a small, leather pouch from the inside lining of his coat, undid the draw-string and removed a small diamond, placed it in front of Bryce, and said. 'You fix it with the authorities and I will take you there.'

26

Bryce looked at the pouch.

Later, in Captain Jonas' cabin, Bryce stood watching as the Captain examined the booty he had extricated from the desperate 'passengers'. He picked up the small diamond Diem had given Bryce and examined it. The stone glistened in his fingers as it caught the light from the desk lamp.

'Not a bad swag, eh?' Bryce said.

Jonas then added it to the rest of the pile of bribes on the desk.

'That's all of it?'

He looked Bryce squarely in the face. Bryce smiled and raised his arms in innocence.

'Have you ever known me to hold out on the organisation?'

Jonas started to collect the valuables together, putting them in a large envelope as he spoke, 'Only because you know we check.'

Bryce chuckled and said, 'The extra information I pick up from the Gooks should be worth a little incentive, surely?'

Jonas locked the envelope in his safe.

'So go and see the big man when you get back ashore. Maybe he'll give you a bonus.'

The sullen refugees watched as Bryce, Jonas and Brandwell made their way along the deck to the ladder leading down to the Patrol launch. The boat's engine kicked into life as soon as the trio arrived causing them to almost shout their conversation. Diem translated for the others.

'If you do decide to dock in Australian waters,' Bryce shouted to Jonas, 'I warn you, the Immigration boys will be waiting for you, Captain. And frankly, from my preliminary interviews, I can tell you now there's not one of your *passengers* that's got Buckley's chance of getting their entry papers.'

Jonas, matching Bryce's volume, shouted back angrily. 'And what the hell am I supposed to do with them?'

'You're aware of the regulations, Captain. They'll be held in detention until they're processed in probably a couple of years' time or you will be guarded while you refuel and take them back where they came from.'

Dismissing any further conversation, Bryce saluted and disappeared down the ladder followed by his crew attendants.

As the patrol launch sped off back towards shore, the refugees began to advance menacingly on Jonas and Bryce but the sudden clicks of automatic weapons held by the crew stopped them in their tracks. A tense silence settled over the deck as Jonas spat out an order to Brandwell.

'Mr Brandwell, escort all of the passengers to the mess dining room, please. I have an announcement to make.'

He then strode off leaving Brandwell and the crew very much in command of the situation.

With the angry refugees assembled in what was laughingly called the 'dining room', which in fact was a dingy, dirty area set aside below decks, with chipped laminated tables and grubby, vinyl chairs, Jonas stood on one of the tables, flanked by a couple of armed guards. Several other armed crew stood guard at the entrance.

'So as illegal immigrants, it's pretty clear what the authorities' attitude is going to be if you fall into their hands: detention camps, interrogations, and eventually, deportation.'

This brought an infuriated outburst from the refugees and the guards stepped in, raising their weapons threateningly.

'But,' Jonas shouted above the uproar, 'the organisation guaranteed you safe arrival and we have a contingency plan in place that will fulfil our guarantee, if you agree.'

This completely silenced the crowd who looked at each other, speculatively, as they strained to hear this new revelation.

'In a few hours' time, after dark, a fishing trawler will pull alongside. You will transfer into it and be taken into a remote bay on the mainland. You will be met and transferred by trucks, first to safe farm houses, and then to various destinations controlled by our organisation. There you will be offered work, suitable to your qualifications. Those who take advantage of our offer will be issued with entry permits and visas. You will be looked after and protected from the authorities in return for your loyalty and co-operation to the organisation.'

A silence settled over the refugees as they considered the proposal.

Brandwell appeared at the entrance and, catching Jonas' eye, signalled him to meet him in the corridor. As Jonas was helped down from the table, Diem stood and raising his voice and an arm, called out, 'This all sounds very dangerous, Captain, and forgive me for saying, but it would appear that, if we agree with your proposal, we will forever be under the control of your … organisation – as slaves. That was not included in the original contract. Would the offer of "work suitable to our qualifications", mean illegal activities and in some cases, prostitution?'

Jonas smiled around the room and said, 'In your case, I don't think the latter would be a viable option, Mr. Diem.'

This brought a laugh from some of the refugees and lowered the tension in the room.

Someone else spoke up, addressing the gathering. 'We were all aware of the possible dangers when we agreed to this trip. We are all illegal refugees and as such, have to take our chances. Nobody can guarantee the future and forever is a long time. Much can happen, and Australia is a big country with a big coastline. They cannot patrol it all the time.'

As Jonas left the room he called out, 'I'll give you a couple of minutes to think it over. Only those who agree to work for the organisation will be given protection and issued with papers.'

The other refugees fell into excitedly discussing the situation as Jonas made his way out of the room and into the corridor where he joined Brandwell.

'What's up?' Jonas said.

'We've got a problem,' Brandwell replied.

Sweating, delirious and having difficulty breathing, Mrs Diem lay in pain and almost unconscious on one of the grubby bunks. A thin, worn blanket had been thrown over her. Jonas, Brandwell and a young spotty-faced medical orderly, Terry, stood looking down at her.

'Looks like typhoid,' Brandwell muttered.

Jonas' face darkened as he turned to the young, nervous medic. 'What do you think?'

Terry was inexperienced and obviously under a lot of strain as he replied uncertainly, 'Could be, I suppose.'

'But you don't *know?*'

'Look, I was a medical orderly, not a friggin' doctor! The only training I had was a couple of stinkin' months in the Army before the end.'

Jonas' glare brought the young man back under control.

'Was that before or after you deserted?'

Terry sighed and calmed down. 'She's got the symptoms – fever, blotches on her chest and stomach, severe pains – I saw a case in 'Nam. It looks the same.'

Jonas turned to Brandwell. 'We've been weeks at sea. Why didn't it show up before this?'

Brandwell shrugged.

'Maybe she didn't have it when she boarded. Maybe there's a carrier on board.'

This was one suggestion Jonas could have done without. If there was a breakout of typhoid, it would mean panic and maybe many unplanned burials at sea.

He turned to Terry.

'Okay, son, you're relieved. We'll take care of this.'

Terry turned from one to the other knowing full well what was being inferred.

'You heard the Captain,' snarled Brandwell, 'beat it.'

Relieved at his dismissal, Terry hurried from the cabin but before he could reach the door, Brandwell added, 'And keep your mouth shut about this.'

Terry nodded and gratefully escaped.

Jonas turned to Brandwell who said, 'The old man let it out to Bryce that she was also an advanced tubercular.' After a thoughtful pause he added with a look of calm resignation, 'So that's it then. She can't go ashore.'

Jonas nodded his head in reluctant agreement. 'Pity. I hoped this one would be a tidy trip. See to it,' he said brusquely as he exited the cabin, closing the door after him.

Brandwell looked down at the frail old lady as he removed his leather belt. Looping it to form a noose, he slowly advanced towards her.

The buzz of conversation continued as Jonas entered the dining room and moved to the front to address the refugees.

'Right,' he said, 'we haven't got much time. Is there anyone who is not interested in working for the organisation?'

He paused to look around but no one raised their hand. Diem leant across to Hoang who was sitting next to him and whispered, 'You will accept their offer?'

Hoang smiled cynically. 'There is an option?'

Almost to himself Diem replied, 'No … No option.'

There were no dissenters.

'Good,' said Jonas. 'Now, if you'll all return to your quarters and get your belongings together – And oh, by the way, just a formality – is there anyone whose inoculations aren't up to date? – smallpox, cholera, typhoid?'

Surprisingly, only one person raised his hand: Hoang.

'But we do not need them coming into Australia,' he said.

'It's just a safety precaution, Mr Hoang,' Jonas smiled. 'Which are overdue?'

'All of them,' Hoang replied.

'Not a problem, Mr Hoang, I'll send Mr Brandwell down to you in a little while. He'll take you to the infirmary.' He looked around the gathering. 'Anyone else?'

If there was, no one was admitting to it.

'Right, return to your quarters' – which of course meant the hold – 'and get your things together.'

31

Excited, the refugees stood and began to exit noisily passing Brandwell who pushed his way through them. Jonas raised an eyebrow, silently questioning him if the 'job' was done. Brandwell nodded in confirmation. Old Mr Diem was the last to leave and Jonas stopped him on his way out.

'Oh, Mr Diem.'

Diem stopped and turned back, a little nervous at being singled out.

'Yes, Captain?'

Looking suitably disturbed, Jonas said, 'I'm afraid I have some rather bad news for you.'

Diem looked alarmed. 'You are not going to allow my wife and me ashore?'

'No, it's not that. But it is about your wife.'

A touch of fear appeared in the old man's face as Jonas continued.

'She was a lot worse than we thought. It appears she had typhoid. But I think you realised that, didn't you?'

His suspicions now confirmed, Diem's face creased in pain. But then he realised that the captain was talking in the past tense.

'Had? You said, had?

Jonas again raised the mask of concern and replied gently, 'Your wife died a few minutes ago ... I'm sorry.'

For a moment it looked as if Diem was going to collapse but he managed to regain his control. There was a long pause before the old man could speak.

'I – I did not know for sure ... The trip has been very hard on her ... I thought ... if I could just get her ashore ... I could get proper treatment for her ...'

His voice trailed off into shocked silence. Jonas placed what appeared to be a sympathetic hand on his shoulder.

'I know, it's hard. But under the circumstances, you realise she'll have to be buried at sea?'

But Diem didn't want to think about that just yet.

'I would like to see her,' he said as he tried to pass Jonas.

'I don't think that would be a good idea,' Jonas said, restraining the old man with a firm hand on his arm.

'We have been married for almost forty years,' Diem said with great dignity. 'I must say my farewells.'

Jonas shot a look at Brandwell and drew him aside. The two men whispered for a few moments and Brandwell left the room. Jonas returned to Diem.

'Alright, Mr Diem, Mr Brandwell will attend to it. Follow me.'

Still in shock, Diem nodded vaguely and followed Jonas out.

Brandwell was just finishing covering Mrs Diem with the rug when there was a knock on the door and it opened to reveal Jonas standing in the doorway. Jonas raised his eyebrows, silently questioning if all was in order and Brandwell nodded. Jonas stood aside and Diem entered and made his way to the bedside. Tears welled in his eyes and tumbled down his aged cheeks as he stood looking down at the face of his dead wife. The rug had been arranged so that only her face was visible. Diem turned to Jonas and said, 'May I have a moment alone with my wife, please?'

Brandwell was hesitant but Jonas took control saying, 'I wouldn't touch her, Mr Diem, under the circumstances. You must leave the rug covering her.'

Diem nodded and Jonas pulled Brandwell a few steps away to the back of the room and whispered to him, ignoring the old man's suffering.

'You've got another one to take care of.'

Brandwell looked up sharply, waiting for his next instruction.

'Hoang – I think he's the carrier,' Jonas whispered.

'What's the point, he'll be ashore in a couple of hours,' Brandwell whispered back.

'And liable to start an epidemic in the camps. Do you realise what that would mean?'

'You don't think two sudden deaths might look a bit suss?' said Brandwell.

'I'll handle that. You just do your job – quietly,' was the reply.

While Jonas and Brandwell were whispering together, Diem started to pray quietly by his wife's body. With tears trickling down his already wet cheeks, he gradually sank to his knees, and in the process, accidentally dragged the rug away from the top section of his dead wife's body, revealing the ugly red welts and bruises around her throat made by Brandwell's belt as he strangled her.

This went unnoticed by the captain and his mate who were immersed in whispered conversation. Diem raised his eyes to look at his wife's face and slowly, through the haze of sadness, began to notice the welts and bruising. At first puzzled and then with growing horror, he slowly became fully aware of what had happened. With the awakening of full realisation, his face became a frozen mask of disbelief and revulsion which gradually turned to hate.

For several seconds he remained frozen as the full ramifications sank in. Suddenly he realised that if he revealed this knowledge, he would never leave the cabin alive. Slowly he stood up and covered his dead wife's face with the stained and dirty rug. After one last look he forced himself to revert back to the grieving husband, gathered his strength and walked slowly out of the cabin, without trusting himself to spare a sideways glance at his wife's murderers. Jonas and Brandwell watched him leave, not knowing that their crime had been discovered.

*

Lying just beyond the twelve-mile limit, an old fishing trawler, with her name, the *Shark*, painted on her hull, met the *Luger* at the prearranged time and hove to. Bathed in pale moonlight in the relatively calm water, both vessels soon became a hive of quiet activity. Helped by the *Luger's* crew, the refugees and their meagre belongings were soon being transferred aboard the *Shark*.

Standing in line waiting for his turn to board, Diem stood at the rail looking towards the rugged, wooded and unlit coastline. Jonas approached and handed him an envelope.

'I forgot to give you your papers, Mr Diem.'

Diem came out of his reverie and turned to Jonas. The shadows covered the loathing on the old man's face as he took the envelope and tucked it in his overcoat pocket.

'I thought we would not receive them until we arrived on shore.'

'This will save you some time,' Jonas smiled. 'I don't expect you'll try to run away. You will be landing at a very remote area. You'd better get on board the trawler.'

Diem studied his face, carefully remembering every feature for future identification. And he was determined there would be a need when these monsters were finally brought to justice.

Jonas held out his hand. 'Good luck in your new life – and your new job.'

Completely ignoring the gesture, Diem picked up his battered suitcase and moved to the ladder. He turned to descend and paused, looking Jonas full in the face.

'I'll never forget what you have done, Captain,' he said calmly.

Jonas took this in a manner not quite as it was intended and replied, 'Try – for your own sake.'

Just as Diem disappeared down the ladder, Brandwell appeared at Jonas' side. Jonas turned to him and said, 'All done?'

Brandwell nodded. 'He hardly felt a thing.'

Jonas acknowledged and turned to move off.

'Stand by to get underway as soon as the trawler shoves off.'

'Dump the bodies the same as before?' asked Brandwell.

Another nod from Jonas. 'And make sure they're well weighted this time.'

'I'll exchange his money-belt for a few heavy chains,' Brandwell smirked. 'They'll sink quicker.'

'And make sure you hand the money belt and its contents over to me,' the captain added with a barely concealed threat.

'Naturally, sir,' Brandwell replied with a slight sneer and a patronising salute.

Brandwell moved off just as Hooker, the skipper of the *Shark*, arrived at Jonas' side. He was a short, rugged, unpleasant man in his mid forties who smelled of sweat, fish and the sea. He carried a fish basket stacked with plastic bags filled with white powder.

'Just about ready, Captain,' he said in a coarse Australian accent.

'Right, skipper, you got the stuff, I see.'

Hooker smiled and held up the basket in confirmation.

'If that rusty old tub of yours goes down on the way back,' Jonas continued, 'make sure you save that before any of the passengers.'

Hooker laughed harshly, 'Don't worry, Captain, if the *Shark* goes down I'll stuff this lot up me arse and swim ashore.'

'Stuff that lot up your arse,' Jonas smiled, 'and you won't need to swim – You'll fucking well fly.'

Hooker laughed again and moved off to board the trawler.

'See ya next trip.'

Jonas gave a mock salute and watched as the *Shark's* engines caught, the restraining ropes were released, and the fishing trawler pulled silently away heading for the dark coastline. On board the refugees sat huddled together uncomfortably, more for some kind of mutual reassurance than the lack of room. Diem stood alone in the stern watching the *Luger* and his past fade into the night. But it was revenge that dominated his mind.

Chapter 6

Steve and Tan walked along the street from the car park, heading for their local pub. Both were in a light-hearted mood, chatting and occasionally laughing as they joshed with each other.

'Now remember,' Steve said, 'whatever happens, don't let me get pissed.'

Tan laughed.

'I've heard that one before. You know I can't stop you, nobody can.'

'No, I mean it, not tonight.'

'You have been pretty good lately though,' Tan admitted. 'Not so ugly.'

'I never got ugly with you,' Steve objected.

'No, not with me,' Tan replied; 'that's because you needed me to carry you home.'

Steve laughed and playfully slapped Tan across the back of his head as they entered the pub.

*

The shoreline was dark as the *Shark* pulled alongside a rickety jetty set on the narrow, pebbled beach. The shadows from the nearby gum trees and bush engulfed the scene in semi-darkness. Strange bush noises assailed the newcomers' ears and created an eerie atmosphere filled with the fear of the unknown. A mother and her two small children were assisted from the launch and, missing their footing, fell into the dark water. The children screamed as they floundered and two of the crew jumped into the water to assist them.

'Shut those bloody kids up!' Hooker hissed.

The two sailors grabbed the panic-stricken family and unceremoniously dragged them onto the shore and up onto the bank. Soaking wet, the mother and children struggled to free themselves as they were forcibly pushed to join the other passengers as they made their way to a small clearing that surrounded the approach to the jetty.

When they were all ashore and gathered in a ragged group, Hooker stood in front of them and spoke quietly but urgently.

'Right, there's to be no lights, no talking, and as little noise as possible.'

Two ex-military trucks were parked nearby and they briefly flashed the headlights.

'You'll be broken into two groups and loaded into those trucks so those who want to stick together, organise yourselves now. You will be going to different locations. And we haven't got time for fond farewells, so let's move it!'

'Excuse me, Captain,' said Diem, 'where are we now and where are you taking us?'

'We're in a remote area near the South Australian border. We're takin' you to a farmhouse not far from here,' Hooker replied. 'They'll give you a meal and bed ya down for a few hours, then you'll be split up and moved on. Now, no more talkin' – get in.' As an afterthought, he added, 'And watch y'self, gran'pa, don't fall out.'

The refugees were loaded into the back of the trucks and the drivers pulled down canvas flaps, climbed behind the wheel and started their engines. The first truck turned onto a dirt track and with its lights on low beam, slowly made its way through the scrub. Diem, who was in the second truck, urgently whispered in Vietnamese to the man next to him, 'I cannot go, cover for me.'

Without waiting for a reply, he grabbed his suitcase, pushed it through the canvas flap and followed it, jumping to the ground just as the truck started to move off. Scrambling to his feet he quickly hid in the underbrush.

The low growl of the trucks faded into the darkness. When all was quiet again, Diem stepped out of the bush and looked in the direction the trucks had taken.

For a moment he stood, taking in his predicament, and then he removed a small torch and a compass from his overcoat pocket. With the aid of the dim torchlight, he studied the compass and decided on the direction he needed to take. Pulling his overcoat around him to help protect him from the cold night air, he picked up his suitcase and resolutely began to walk up the bush track.

*

Steve and Tan entered the rowdy, crowded bar. Steve's ex-Nam comrades, the gaunt Splicer, the lean, sandy- haired Finch, and the short, one-armed Joey, all part of his support group and his usual drinking partners, gave them a raucous welcome. Steve and Tan waved back in greeting.

'Ah, if it isn't Australia's Steve Saunders, the Vung Tau Terror, and his faithful manservant, Tan, the Phuoc Tuy Fucker,' Finch called out.

'G'day, Steve, Tan,' yelled Joey, and held up two fingers of his one remaining hand to the bar girl. 'Hey, Josie – two beers, love.'

'Better make that three,' Splicer added.

Joey held up three fingers.

'Four,' Finch called.

Joey held up four fingers and then looked down at his own half-empty glass and laughed. 'Oh, what the hell, I'm celebrating, make that five,' he said as he again changed the number of fingers.

'Nobody make it six,' Finch yelled, 'Joey will have to drop his daks.'

The other four laughed and Splicer added dryly, 'Only if they order a middy,' which got an even bigger laugh. He then turned to Steve.

'And how's me lovely little Su-Su?'

'Just like her Saigon bar-girl namesake,' Steve replied, 'fucked.'

The others laughed but Splicer was not fazed. 'That's when Saigon Su-Su performed best,' he sighed wistfully.

'That's what all the GI grunts used to say,' Steve smiled as he downed half of his beer.

'I'll have you know,' Splicer said indignantly, 'she was untouched by human hands when I found her.'

'And she still was when you left her,' laughed Joey, which brought a howl of agreement from the others.

'They tell me,' Finch said, conspiratorially, 'they've got her up in Canberra now, in a Defence Department filing cabinet. She's the only complete set of records they've got of every vets' finger prints.'

Splicer stood up to his full six foot two of injured dignity.

'The trouble with you bastards,' he said, 'is ya got no class.' Turning to the barmaid he shouted, 'Hey, Josie, where's the shovel? I gotta go to the bog.'

The others laughed as Splicer weaved his way to the toilets.

'Don't mind Splicer, Josie,' Steve said, 'he's still not used to flushing toilets.'

'No,' chipped in Joey, 'when he first got back, he thought they were new-fangled washing machines.'

Not to be outdone, Finch added, 'He kept runnin' downstairs to see where his clothes were disappearin' to.'

The others laughed but Josie gave them a you've-told-me-that-one-a-dozen-times-before look and moved off down the bar to serve another customer.

Deflated, Finch looked at the others.

'We've gotta change our bar.'

*

Sally was preparing dinner, moving around the small kitchen with ease, everything close at hand. She'd only moved into

Steve's small Victorian cottage a few months ago and had already transformed the place from what it was when she'd moved in: a typical bachelor pad that Steve used for sleeping, showering and storage, and eating the occasional take-away meal. Housework and comfort weren't a priority then. His laundry, when he remembered, was run through the local laundromat, and the few pot plants had died long ago from neglect.

Now, after only a short time, Sally had set to work and turned the place into a home. The interior had been painted off-white with natural timber trim, she'd torn down the ragged curtains and replaced them with shutters, re-designed and modernised the kitchen and bathroom, and decorated the place with fresh pot plants and a mixture of new and period pieces that gave a comfortable, lived-in look. Even surprising herself, she had become quite house-proud and was continually picking things up from secondhand shops and restoring them into pieces that really made a difference to the ambience and comfort.

This had certainly not been a part of her long-term plan but meeting Steve and falling in love with him had certainly put aside any ambitions of using her PhD in psychology to become a full partner in Robert Heston's clinic.

Unknown to Steve, Heston had originally asked her to 'take him under her wing' and see if she could help him with his Post Trauma Stress condition. She had eagerly accepted, under the condition that Steve was not to know of her affiliation with Heston, thinking she could attack the problem better if he didn't know of their relationship. But what started as an interesting psychological experiment finished up a heart- and life-changing experience.

It had all started quite naturally when Heston secretly arranged for them to meet *accidentally* at one of his parties, but there was an immediate attraction and against her strong principles of not becoming emotionally involved with a patient, especially a Post Trauma case, she gradually came to realise that, despite her reluctance, she was falling in love with him.

Although she tried to extricate herself from the relationship several times and pull back emotionally, her attraction to him, which was very definitely reciprocated, became too strong to fight and she eventually succumbed to his natural charm. The fact that he was also a devastatingly attractive, masculine, yet vulnerable man, with the body of a Greek god, didn't do any harm either.

She talked to him and, more importantly, encouraged him to talk to her. She secretly counselled him without him knowing he was being counselled, and gently led him away from many of his demons and eventually won his trust. There had been some rough times but their love for each other helped get them through.

There was a sudden knock at the front door and Sally assumed it was Steve playing a joke on her, which was not uncommon. She threw the tea towel down on the bench, patted her hair in place, checked her makeup in the little Victorian mirror in the hall, opened the door and stood in a seductive pose, leaning against the door frame with an arm above her shoulder, resting her hand high on the wall. To her embarrassment, standing on the little porch was a blonde woman in her early thirties. Although attractive she looked a little drawn and older than her years. Her simple grey frock hinted at better times. Her blue eyes appeared a little nervous and her voice was tiny and quiet as she said, 'Oh', somewhat in surprise. 'Does Steve Saunders still live here?'

Sally hastily relaxed from her sexy pose.

'Yes, he does but I'm sorry, he …'

'Could I see him, please?' the woman cut in. 'I'm Ann Saunders. His wife … or rather, his ex-wife.'

Somewhat taken aback herself, and wondering how to handle this new and surprising development, Sally stuttered, 'Oh … I see … Won't you come in?'

*

In the bar, Steve, Tan, Finch and Joey still stood at the bar drinking. Steve handed Tan another beer while he said to Joey, 'Did you say you were celebrating before?'

Joey smiled. 'Yeah, I got a job – Public Service Records.'

'Hey, that's great,' said Steve. 'When did you hear?'

'Just today. Personnel manager said there was nothin' to it. He said I could do it with one hand tied behind me back. Then he looked at me stump and realised what he'd said.'

The four men laughed.

'I pissed meself,' Joey laughed, 'and I said, "Jesus, just as well".'

They all laughed again.

At that moment, a group of four tough-looking merchant navy types entered the bar. One of them was a particularly vicious-looking thug by the name of Pete Ricketts. He was a heavy, big-shouldered man in his late thirties, with a pock-marked face that almost camouflaged the scar on his wide jaw. His eyes were small and dark. The four men made their way to the other end of the bar and ordered beers.

'Christ, look what just walked in.' Finch whispered to the others.

At that point Ricketts was in conversation with his mates and hadn't noticed Steve's group. A sudden silence fell on the ex-Nam vets broken only by a low growl from Joey.

'Shit – Ricketts. Pete Ricketts.' Steve turned to look and the smile died on his face.

'Who's Pete Ricketts?' Tan asked.

'Fuckin' sergeant in our unit,' Finch replied, 'a right bastard.'

The colour had drained from Steve's face and his mind was unwillingly thrown back into the past. Subliminal flashes of Ricketts, in army jungle gear, his face smeared with camouflage grease, grinning sadistically as he moved through the stinking, humid jungle; Ricketts' face distorted with bloodlust as he screamed like an attacking madman; and a third flash of Ricketts' face, as it was spattered with a gush of blood from a bayoneted victim, the blood spurting into his eyes and mouth, and him smiling like it was mother's milk. Steve blinked trying to force the memories back into the recesses of his tortured mind.

Tan shot a worried look at Steve.

'Steve?'

Steve snapped himself back under control and gave Tan a haunted look.

'You alright?' Tan asked.

'Yeah, sure,' Steve replied, shaking his head and pushing the fear even further into the abyss. He grinned unconvincingly, and automatically put a protective arm around Tan's shoulders and turned back to the bar.

'I thought he'd bought it,' Joey said.

'Wishful fuckin' thinking, ' Finch snarled. 'He liked it so much he signed up for a third tour. I haven't seen him since ...' His voice trailed off as he met Steve's eyes.

'Suoi Luc,' Steve said softly. 'The last patrol.'

There was an awkward silence with each of the vets lost in their own individual memories. Tan watched Steve with growing apprehension. Suddenly Steve finished his beer and turned to him.

'I think I'll push off – coming?'

Tan swamped the last of his beer. 'Yeah.'

'See you boys tomorrow,' Steve said, placing his empty glass on the bar beside Tan's.

'Yeah, right, see ya, Steve, Tan,' the others chorused.

Steve led the way to the exit but to do so he had to pass Ricketts and his mates. Ricketts glanced up and caught sight of them, doing a double take in his surprise. His face broke into an evil amiable grin as he stepped into Steve's path.

'Well, I'll be buggered! Steve Saunders!'

Steve sighed and was forced to stop.

'G'day, Pete.'

To an outsider, Ricketts appeared to be pleased to see him. Steve was dangerously cool.

'Bloody hell,' said Ricketts. 'How've ya been? Have a beer.'

'No thanks,' Steve declined as he tried to step around him.

But Ricketts took another step, blocking his way.

'What are you doin' with yourself nowadays?'

Steve replied calmly, 'I own a garage up the road.'

'Get away! Still see any of the boys?'

'Sometimes. Thought you'd still be in the army.'

Ricketts barked a laugh, 'No friggin way. I stayed there till the end. When the fun stopped I got as far away from foot-sloggin' as I could. I joined up with the merchant navy. Just in town to meet up with the ship.' He slapped Steve on the back. His touch made Steve's stomach cringe. 'Sure you won't have a beer?'

'No, we're just going.'

For the first time Ricketts noticed Tan standing behind Steve and scowled, his expression hardening.

'Are you with him?' he asked incredulously.

'Yeah,' Steve replied, casually putting a protective hand on Tan's shoulder.

Suddenly Ricketts laughed harshly. 'Jesus, I thought even you would've had enough of them by now. What'd ya do, bring him back as a pet – a souvenir?'

Tan could feel Steve's arm muscles go rigid on his shoulders.

'You shouldn't let him outta his cage though.'

He turned to share the joke with his mates and Steve suddenly tensed and clenched his fists but Tan restrained him.

'No, Steve, don't throw away the last twelve months.'

Ricketts turned back with a sneer, waiting for a response from Steve.

At the bar, Joey and Finch put their beers down on the counter, preparing to go to their mate's assistance.

For a long moment it looked like Steve was going to ignore Tan's advice but he gradually relaxed and the tension seemed to ease. He even managed a smile.

'You haven't changed, have you, Pete?'

He turned and walked out of the pub, closely followed by Tan.

Ricketts watched them go, speculatively, and then turned back to his mates.

Joey and Finch, the threat of a punch-up diminished, picked up their beers and continued drinking.

Steve and Tan exited from the pub, Steve's temper still inwardly boiling as they made their way to the car park.

'See you tomorrow,' Tan said.

'Yeah,' Steve grunted.

Tan stopped and looked at his friend.

'Steve, forget it. I know how hard it was but you did the right thing. He's not worth it.'

Steve almost seemed to throw off his anger and smiled ruefully.

'Or the risk. Did you see those big bastards with him?'

Tan laughed.

'They would have made mincemeat out of both of us.'

Steve laughed back.

'Yeah, a gimp and a skinny kid – great odds! Thanks for holding me back.'

They both laughed and Steve raised his arm in farewell.

'Well, see you in the morning.'

'Right,' called Tan as he watched Steve get into his car.

He deliberately waited until Steve started his engine and pulled out into the traffic, and then returned to his own car and drove away in the opposite direction.

Steve checked his rear-view mirror and, seeing he wasn't being followed, made a sudden left turn into a side street and pulled into the kerb. He parked the car, got out, and slammed the door behind him. He stood for a moment looking back towards the pub and then strode off in that direction. He wasn't finished with Ricketts yet.

Chapter 7

Ann wandered around Steve and Sally's living room, looking the place over. She glanced into the bedroom and was surprised to see only one queen-sized bed. When she and Steve were married they'd had twin beds because after Steve came back from 'Nam, sometimes he'd had uncontrollable trembling and night sweating and terrible, violent nightmares, and they were forced to sleep separately in case he lashed out and hurt her.

At the large, carved, wooden sideboard she came across a collection of photographs framed in brass. She picked up one of Steve and Sally, smiling happily on a bush picnic. The background was slightly blurred, which gave more emphasis to the smiling faces. Another photograph showed the two lovers on the deck of Steve's boat, the *Long Tall Sally*. Ann noticed the name, which confirmed the relationship was obviously a long and committed one.

Sally came back from the kitchen carrying a tray with a coffee pot and cups as Ann returned the photographs to their place. She was still nervous being in unfamiliar territory.

'This is very nice ... the house, I mean. A bit different to the way we ... Steve used to live.'

'Thanks,' Sally smiled. 'I think you'll find he's changed a lot in the last few years ... Black, you said?' indicating the coffee pot.

Ann nodded and moved to a chair by the coffee table. There was an uncomfortable pause as the two women settled themselves, smiling uncertainly.

'Look,' Ann finally said, 'I didn't come here to make trouble. I'll just have this and go. It was silly my coming here after all this time. I just thought ...' Her voice trailed away, not quite knowing what she thought. 'I should've known he'd have ... someone else ...'

Again the voice trailed off and she grinned uncomfortably. 'Awkward, isn't it?'

Sally smiled in agreement, and relaxed a little. 'As you say, it's been a long time. How long, exactly?'

'Well over two years,' Ann replied soberly.

She tried to save the situation by brightening up.

'I just thought I'd drop in and say hello,' she said nervously.

'I'm only passing through ... on my way back to Queensland ... My boyfriend is waiting for me back at the hotel,' she lied, attempting to diffuse any misunderstanding on Sally's part that she still considered Steve as a part of her life.

'I take it there were no children?' Sally asked, gently.

Ann shook her head.

'No, thank God. Steve and I were what you'd call childhood sweethearts.' She smiled ruefully. 'We grew up together in a small farming area up north. Our parents were friends. Steve's father was a bit strange too. He was a soldier in the Second World War and his mother told my mother that he came back a different man too.'

She tried to mentally equate this but wasn't really up to it so she changed tack and brightened.

'Steve was mad on cameras and films and he had a passion for boats, of all things.'

She laughed nervously and glanced over at the photograph of the *Long Tall Sally*.

'And, as you can imagine, there wasn't a lot offering for those sorts of things in a rural area. We were both determined to get out and make something of our lives. We moved to the big smoke and Steve got a job at the *Herald* newspaper as a trainee television news cameraman. He was very good at it. I worked as a waitress. We were only married just before Steve left for Vietnam on an assignment and when he came back ...'

The rest she left unsaid.

Sally nodded, and tried to change the subject.

'Well, Steve shouldn't be too long if you'd like to wait. He's just down the pub having a few drinks with his mates.'

Ann's attitude changed as she pulled herself together and sat just a little more rigidly.

'Oh, well, in that case, I definitely won't wait. I know how long that can take.'

Sally was surprised at this sudden change. 'Pardon?'

'How do you cope with it?' Ann couldn't stop herself from asking sympathetically. 'Obviously better than I did.'

'Steve doesn't have a drinking problem, Ann, if that's what you mean.'

Ann almost scoffed, 'Well, you're lucky. It used to give him a terrible temper. He used to just … lash out. You never knew when he was going to explode.'

'That was after he came back from Vietnam?' asked Sally.

Ann nodded sadly at the memory.

'He was completely changed. Of course, he had been wounded. But even after he got better he was never the same.'

'I don't think any of them were,' Sally said. 'Did he ever talk to you about it?'

Ann shook her head.

'He didn't want to, but that was alright. I knew it would take him a while to settle down. Then sometimes he'd start to tell me things but it all sounded pretty awful so I had to stop him. It had happened and he just had to get over it and forget about it. There was no point in dragging it all up again. Soldiers from other wars had to do it. Life had to go on. But it didn't.'

Sally desperately wanted to remonstrate with her and defend Steve but realised that it would be of little use, or comfort. Ann was the kind who believed war and suffering were exclusively a man's domain and it shouldn't interfere with his home life or his wife. And if it did, it was his job to fix it.

'It must have been a hard time … for both of you,' Sally said sadly, understanding the tragedy that had broken up so many marriages.

Ann looked at her uncomfortably and nodded.

*

Away from the bar, Splicer was seriously chatting up a rather plain-looking girl, but it appeared, even in her desperation, she wasn't interested. This wasn't conceivable as far as he was concerned and he continued to turn on what he thought of as charm, knowing sooner or later she would surely succumb to his attractions. Intent on his mission, he didn't notice Steve arrive back in the pub and join Ricketts and his friends, drinking, smiling and chatting as if they were long-lost buddies. Further down the bar, Joey and Finch watched disbelievingly as Steve laughed at something Ricketts had said.

'Sorry I was a bit uptight before, Pete,' Steve was saying. 'I've got a bit of a soft spot for the little gook. Y'see, he saved my life when he was just a kid, back in 'Nam.'

'Oh, how did he do that,' Ricketts smiled. 'Stop ya from drinkin' the water?'

They both laughed appreciatively and Steve continued.

'Nah, it must've been after you left your unit. To tell you the truth, everything that happened over there is still a bit blurry. All I can remember is I was pretty badly wounded and in a bit of shock so they told me afterwards. Apparently I got left behind after I'd been wounded in a fire fight out on patrol one day.' He shook his head as if trying to remember the details but failing.

'Place was crawling with VC. When it was all over, Tan found me and dragged me back to his village.'

Ricketts watched him closely, feigning interest.

'He was just a young kid but somehow he managed to patch me up and hide me from Charlie until they had cleared out of the area. Then he put me in a cart somehow and pushed me all the way back to the base hospital. He stuck with me all the time. He hardly left my side they told me, until I was shipped out. The medics reckon I wouldn't have pulled through without him.'

'So, how much did ya have to pay him?' Ricketts asked cynically.

Steve smiled.

'Nothing. Hard to believe, eh?'

'And how did he get out here?'

'He was one of the early boat people.'

'Uh huh, and he got in touch with you and you sponsored him, looked after him and gave him a job, right?'

'Yeah, something like that.'

'And you reckon you didn't pay him for saving your life? What d'you think you're doin' now?'

Steve smiled as if in 'newly discovered' understanding.

'I never thought of it like that.'

'There's always a payoff with them, son.'

There was a sudden uproar from the other side of the bar when the plain subject of Splicer's desire had had enough and suddenly roared at him and kneed him in the groin. Splicer yelled and clutched himself as if he was giving birth to twins and sank to the floor.

'I am not your *little girlie*,' she screamed at him, 'and I don't want a root, and, not that it's any of your business, but I happen to be a lesbian and I'm waiting for my girlfriend! So piss off!'

The bar erupted in laughter and Steve had to raise his voice for Ricketts to hear.

'Hey, we've got a lot to catch up on. Let's split. There's a quieter place around the corner I usually go to.'

'Right.' Ricketts downed the last of his beer and turned to his mates. 'Listen, me and me old army buddy are shovin' off. See ya at the wharf tomorrow.'

His mates nodded and went back to their conversation.

Joey and Finch walked over to the groaning Splicer and helped him to his feet.

'Trust you, Splicer, to pick on a dyke,' said Finch. 'I hope you didn't ask her to marry you. Don't want her girlfriend comin' after you with her lead dildo.'

But Joey was puzzled as he watched Steve and Ricketts leave.

They shared a laugh as they walked down the almost deserted street. Ricketts was in the middle of telling Steve one of his favourite combat stories of the war.

'And so I gave her a jab in the guts with me bayonet and out poured this friggin stream of rice! She wasn't pregnant at all! She was smugglin' the bloody stuff out to Charlie!'

Ricketts laughed at the comedy of the situation as they came to the entrance of a narrow lane that opened into the street.

'Hang on,' said Steve, 'let's take the shortcut down here,' and steered Ricketts into the lane.

Ricketts draped a comradely arm over Steve's shoulders as they turned the corner and he continued his story.

'Well, she spun around an' took off like a turd down the sewer. But she didn't get far because …'

Suddenly Ricketts tightened his massive arm around Steve's neck and at the same time smashed a vicious punch into Steve's stomach. Caught completely off guard, Steve's legs buckled. Ricketts grabbed him by the shirtfront and slammed him up against the brick wall of the lane, one arm across Steve's throat. A knife suddenly appeared in Ricketts' other hand and he held it threateningly in front of Steve's face.

'What d'ya take me for, Saunders, a fuckin' greenhorn?'

Steve could hardly breathe, let alone reply.

'You think I can't pick a set-up when I see one?'

'You bastard, Ricketts,' Steve choked.

'My memory's as good as yours, gook-lover. You hated my guts and suddenly you come on like a long, lost buddy.' Steve tried to struggle free but it was useless. 'I remember that patrol.'

'You left me out there for the VC, you fuckin' mongrel,' Steve managed to get out through gritted teeth. 'I was a war correspondent!

'You were a fuckin' cameraman! A Kodak Box Browneye!'

'Stan was killed! You had a duty to get me back – and my tapes!'

'I thought you and your mate had bought it, asshole,' Ricketts hissed. 'I wasn't riskin' the rest of the patrol on a dead fuckin' journo and a cameraman!'

'Pig's arse!' Steve almost screamed in fury. 'You knew what I had on tape. You knew what I had on you! You were saving yourself! You knew what they did to wounded prisoners; the same as you did to them, you slimy shit! The same as you did to that prisoner in Vung Tau! I had that on tape too!'

Suddenly from behind, a tyre lever smashed into Ricketts' knife arm. He screamed in pain and surprise, dropped the knife, staggered and fell to his knees, grabbing his arm. Steve found himself staring into Tan's grinning face.

'Can't leave you alone for a minute, can I?' Tan said.

Steve smiled in relief and choked out, 'You don't trust me.'

He bent down and dragged Ricketts to his feet.

'This is for the *gooks*, Pete,' he said as he smashed a fist into Ricketts' guts. 'And one for Joey's arm, you prick,' as he pounded another punch into his stomach. 'And this one's for leaving me for dead, you vicious fuckin' coward.' He pulled back his arm for another blow but Ricketts recovered enough to slam his fist into Steve's face, the blow glancing off his cheek, and opening a gash that immediately started to bleed.

Although Ricketts now only had one good arm, Steve took no pity on him. He stepped in, blocked a kick aimed at his head, and laid into his opponent, raining punches on Ricketts' head and body mercilessly.

Finch and Joey appeared at the entrance to the lane intending to help Steve but when they saw they weren't really needed, they stood guard, keeping an eye out for intruders. Finally, Steve landed a punch on Ricketts that slammed him against the wall, cracking his head. Unconscious, he slid down the wall to the ground.

Bloodied, breathing heavily, but satisfied, Steve looked down on him.

'God that felt good.'

Tan stepped up to join him. Steve looked at him and smiled. 'Didn't fool you, hey?'

Tan returned the smile.

'I know you too good.'

'Just as well,' Steve said, as he ruffled Tan's hair.

Steve put his arm around Tan's shoulders for support, and they made their way to Finch and Joey waiting at the entrance to the lane.

'Jesus, Steve,' said Finch, 'you could've waited for us.'

'Always the selfish bastard,' said Joey.

Steve smiled and shook his head.

'I don't know – a man can't get any privacy with you lot around.'

The group made their way out into the street.

Chapter 8

In the moonlight, Diem came to an intersection where the dirt track met a highway. He put down his suitcase, again checked his compass and turned to the right along the bitumen road. Behind him lay a long ribbon of deserted highway that disappeared into the darkness and he had no idea how far he would have to walk before he came across any kind of civilisation. And even then, he had no idea what to expect in this strange country. He felt tired but resolute in his determination. He picked up his suitcase and trudged on.

He seemed to have been walking for hours and had sunk into a walking pattern that he had often used in the Vietnamese countryside when he was a much younger man. His mind was well equipped for such a trek, fuelled by the determination to find his son and to rest in his care. Behind him, headlights faintly appeared in the darkness and as they came closer and brighter, he became aware of the sound of an engine. He turned to look and considered he may be able to hitch a lift. The vehicle was obviously a truck, driving slower than one would expect on such a deserted road. But then he noticed a smaller, but more powerful beam of light coming from the driver's cabin, illuminating the bushes and shrubs along either side of the road as if someone was looking for something or someone – maybe for him!

He felt the stirring of panic and desperately looked for cover, maybe a bush or tree trunk, something to hide him from the approaching danger. He began to run frantically looking back over his shoulder. Suddenly something hard slammed painfully into his shoulder, the momentum spinning him around and causing him to drop his suitcase. He stumbled and fell, rolling into a ditch beside the road. He lay in the depression and lifting his head carefully, his eyes just came level with the top of the ditch. He could see his suitcase lying where it fell a few feet away and quickly retrieved it, pulling it back into the ditch just as the truck ambled past, with the powerful torch beam skimming over his hiding place. Unaware of his presence, the vehicle drove on through the night and disappeared around a bend in the road. Shaken and gasping for air, Diem lay in the ditch for a few moments to recover.

Eventually he dragged himself out and back onto the roadside where he got to his feet and retraced his steps to see what had hit him. Taking the small torch from his pocket, he switched it on and flashed the beam around until it came to rest on a signpost standing back from the roadside. He directed the beam upwards until it illuminated a sign that read, 'Nelson 2km'.

*

After the fight, Tan drove Steve home in his souped-up utility. Although a trifle sore, Steve was certainly not sorry, but annoyed that Tan had insisted on driving him home, saying it was totally unnecessary. As they were driving up the street towards Steve's house, Sally was just farewelling Ann on the front porch. Ann said goodnight and walked down the front path, out through the gate and crossed the road to her car as Sally went back inside. Ann stood by her car, which was parked under a tree, just as Tan's utility pulled up outside the house.

Inside the ute's cabin, Steve was still complaining.

'This was really stupid, Tan, I could've driven myself home.'

'Yeah, you've already told me twelve times. We're here, so shut up and get out. Do you want me to come in?'

'No, for Christ's sake, I'm alright!' Steve grumbled to himself as he opened the door. But Tan had got out of the driver's seat and hurried around to help anyway.

'Jesus, Tan!' Steve said caustically, 'I am quite capable of getting myself up the bloody path, goddammit! Go home!'

Tan gave in and smiled. 'I'll pick you up in the morning and we'll get your car.' He returned to the driver's side and got in.

'Tell Sally to ring me if you start to play up and I'll come round and sort you out.'

Steve gave him a nasty hand signal and headed through his front gate.

Ann had recognised Steve in the ute cabin and hurried behind her own car so she wouldn't be seen. She watched the dishevelled, bleeding, belligerent Steve get out, slam the door and make his way to his front door.

Sally had been lying to her, she thought bitterly, Steve hadn't changed at all. She'd seen him arrive home in this state many times. Feeling sad but secretly guilt ridden, she got in her car and drove off.

Tan decided he was hungry after the night's excitement and drove to a Vietnamese cafe in Hawthorn which he had recently discovered and ordered a take-away meal of his home country's delicacies to enjoy in the privacy of his flat. Although he'd been in Australia for years, he still missed much about his homeland but not as it had been when he left it. He'd grown sick of the war and the killing; the lies; the corruption; and his youthful ideals had perished with so many of his family and friends, along with the invaders of both sides. Steve had offered a way out, and when he discovered a group of his fellow disenchanted countrymen were planning to steal a boat and escape, he enthusiastically joined them.

The trip, first to Singapore, where they were arrested and held in detention, was almost as frightening as the war they'd fled from. They were still plagued by hunger, overcrowding, and constant danger. Steve had given him his address when Tan rescued him and took him to the army base hospital in Saigon and stayed on to look after him. Tan was always close by, refusing to leave his damaged Australian friend until he had recovered from the terrible wounds that afflicted him.

Because he looked younger than his age and had a natural boyish charm, which appealed to the medical staff and orderlies, he was almost patronisingly allowed to help look after Steve, washing and feeding him, helping him to take his medicines, reading to him in his almost perfect English, sitting with him in the garden, walking and talking, and generally looking out for him. His presence seemed to have a markedly positive effect on Steve's recovery and they soon became inseparable: the wounded and disturbed news cameraman and the ever-attentive, seemingly hero-struck, Vietnamese orphan.

While detained in Singapore, Tan had become desperate to escape to Australia, determined to somehow contact Steve. He soon discovered six other young men who were also intent on escaping and one night the group broke out, stole a local fishing boat, threw in a few supplies they managed to steal, and set out to sea. It wasn't as easy as the inexperienced sailors had expected. They braved the horrendous seas where waves continually threatened to swamp them, the sun that beat down mercilessly, the storms that lashed them, the hunger and thirst, the boredom of weeks at sea, and were eventually washed ashore, close to death, on the coast of the Northern Territory. The authorities arrested them, of course, and they were taken into custody and put in another detention camp, but with medical aid and good food, they soon recovered and regained their strength.

Tan immediately alerted the authorities to the whereabouts of Steve who was then contacted by the Immigration Department. Steve was overjoyed to hear of the arrival of his young saviour and set the wheels in motion for Tan to be accepted as a legal immigrant whom Steve was more than willing to sponsor. When the full story of Tan's brave devotion was known, official strings were pulled, papers were fast-tracked and very soon he was released into Steve's care. Steve gave him a job in his garage and was surprised at how much knowledge Tan had of engines and mechanics. Their friendship and respect for each other had grown and soon they were again inseparable, easy and content in each other's company, sharing a common background.

By then Steve had been diagnosed as suffering from Post Trauma Stress Syndrome, but Tan was able to help keep him in control to an extent and again to look out for him. Steve reciprocated by becoming over-protective of Tan, which was one of the symptoms of the condition but with which Tan seemed to be able to cope remarkably well.

And now Tan was happy and content as he drove back to his flat, with the delicious aroma of his meal wafting past his nose and filling the cabin of his ute.

Later that night, Sally was sitting at her computer, dressed in her white silk bathrobe, working on the thesis for her Master's Degree, which she had kept secret from Steve, believing he would suspect she was only staying with him for her own ends. It was not coming easily as a deep sense of guilt underlaid her thinking as she tried to push aside her personal feelings. The thesis was entitled 'Continuing Re-adjustment of the Vietnam Veteran'. She didn't want him to read it or even know about it, as it dealt with her personal experience with him. She also didn't want him to think he was constantly being studied as a 'subject' and thereby suspect her love and her motives for being with him.

Steve had gone to bed and was sleeping soundly. After the extreme adrenalin kick from his confrontation with Ricketts, he had slumped. He had showered, Sally had dressed his wounds, and he went to bed early. She had not told him about Ann's visit as there didn't seem any point. Finding out that Steve had been married had surprised her of course, but on the other hand, had fitted into the profile she was constantly building of him.

In the bedroom, a soft glow from the bed lamp illuminated Steve's face. From his expression it was obvious he wasn't sleeping peacefully. His eyes began to flicker under the lids and perspiration began to bead on his forehead. His nightmare suddenly came agonisingly to life like a disjointed, badly edited film. As though through his camera lens, a confused, montage of scenes flashed through his head.

Camouflage-streaked, tense faces of soldiers creeping through the jungle, AK 47s at the ready: Splicer, Finch and Joey, now with both his arms, included in the group, bent low to conceal their presence, watching each other's backs as they pushed through dripping branches and vines. Ricketts' face, different from the others, excited and filled with bloodlust, smiling evilly.

His mind skipped suddenly to shadows and shafts of brilliant sunshine through the jungle canopy, haze and smoke. Sudden explosions, a jungle clearing with rickety shacks, Australian and VC soldiers and peasants, screaming, killing and being killed, splashes and spurts of blood, entrails hacked out of stomachs, butchered limbs lying beside dead or screaming bodies: Ricketts again, bayoneting and slashing, laughing all the time like a madman. The film rolled on, shacks being ignited and bursting into flames, scenes of terror. The nightmare took control and played on in grotesque, disjointed, edited sequences

Ricketts bursting into a shack with weapon blazing, cutting down two peasants, their bodies spasmodically jumping like grotesque puppets as the bullets ripped into them, their young son, a child of about twelve, watching the butchery and screaming in terror. And finally, no longer through a camera lens but as in real life, Steve's nightmare became a horrifying reality as he saw the screaming child stumbling from the burning shack, his arms flailing as he tried desperately and hopelessly to beat out the inferno engulfing him. Steve felt himself running toward the child, trying desperately to save him but as he did, there was a terrible explosion.

From the living room Sally heard a frightening and blood chilling scream.

She flew to the bedroom and was shocked to find Steve sitting bolt upright in bed, eyes staring wildly, trembling and gasping for breath. Instinctively knowing not to go near him when he was in this state, she switched on the overhead light and called out to him, reassuringly. 'Steve! Steve, it's Sally! Listen to me … I'm here … You're safe, I'm with you …It's only a dream.'

She continued to soothe and reassure him until he finally started to calm down and his breathing began to return to almost normal. Only then did she slowly walk towards him continuing to speak calmly and lovingly, 'Darling … It's alright … You're safe … I'm here … I'm with you …'

Eventually his eyes focused on her and his expression began to relax.

She paused, looking at him with deep concern before she spoke.

'Alright?' she whispered soothingly.

Steve nodded and sank back onto the bed and sighed.

'That's the first time for a while,' she said gently as she sat by him on the side of the bed.

He nodded.

'Roll over,' she gently urged him.

With her help he managed to roll over onto his stomach. She expertly began to massage his back and neck and his body slowly started to relax.

'Which one was it?' she asked, when she felt the tension leaving his body.

'Suoi Luc … the big one … my last assignment … Suddenly seeing Ricketts again must've set it off … Fuck him!'

'You know there's always the danger of that happening. But you also know you can deal with it. You're learning to put it into perspective and the power of it will fade. It takes time, Steve, but I know you're getting there. Even Robert is pleased with your improvement.'

Steve rolled over on his back, reached up with his hand and gently stroked her cheek.

'You know, I must be getting better though. A year ago I wouldn't have been able to stop hitting him until I killed him.'

Sally smiled wryly.

'Well, let's be thankful for small mercies.'

They looked lovingly into each other's eyes for a long moment. Sally finally slipped onto the bed next to him, snuggled against him and slipped her arm over his lower stomach. She felt his penis hardening and began to smile.

'You know,' she said, 'you don't have to fake these nightmares, you just have to ask.'

*

Tan, on the other hand, was sleeping peacefully. That was until the phone by his bed rang. He jumped and woke. His immediate reaction was to think that Steve might have had a bad reaction from his encounter with Ricketts, which wouldn't have surprised him, and Sally was ringing him for assistance. Shaking himself alert, he picked up the receiver and an operator's voice said, 'Mr. Nguyen?'

'Yes,' he answered, somewhat relieved.

'I have a reverse charge call for you on the line. Will you accept?'

'Reverse charge?' Tan repeated, puzzled, 'Who is it from, please, and where are they calling from?'

'The caller identifies himself as Mr Nguyen. And he's calling from Nelson, Victoria.'

Fifty percent of Vietnamese are called Nguyen; it's a bit like Smith in English speaking countries and Tan immediately presumed that whoever was ringing was confusing him with one of the other Nguyens. He had no other family in Australia but for politeness' sake he felt he should answer.

'Where is Nelson?' he asked the operator.

'South-western Victoria,' the operator replied, 'near the South Australian border.'

'Are you sure you've got the right number?' Tan asked.

The operator repeated the number and it was certainly Tan's.

This further confused him but he finally relented.

'Alright, operator, I will accept the call.'

The call was connected.

'Hello? Nguyen Tan speaking.'

A man's voice answered in Vietnamese, 'Tan, is that you?'

'Yes,' Tan said, still confused, but slipped into his native tongue and replied, 'Who is calling, please?'

'Tan, this is your father speaking.'

Tan paused in his puzzlement. 'I am sorry, you must be mistaken. My father and mother are in Saigon.'

'No, Tan, it is your father, Diem – Nguyen Diem.'

Tan was shocked into silence for a moment, unable to take it in.

'No, sir, I am terribly sorry but you must be mistaken. There are many Nguyens in the phone book and Tan is also a very common name.'

But the man at the other end of the line would not be diverted.

'Tan, my son, I know it is you. I have your address which you sent me. Listen, when you were a little boy I gave you a pet chicken. His name was Cluck Cluck … You named him Cluck Cluck.'

Tan was utterly dumbfounded. Could this really be his father? No, that would be impossible. He hadn't seen him since he was only a lad when they were separated in the war. Their home had been bombed by the Americans by mistake and his siblings had been killed. Then they had been captured and separated and sent by the Viet Cong to re-education camps. His memories were interrupted by the man's voice on the other end of the line.

'Tan, I am here in Australia. I have made some stupid mistakes. I have become involved with some very bad men. I need your help.'

This suddenly brought Tan's mind back to the present.

'What has happened?' he asked anxiously.

Diem started to tell him the story of his escape from Vietnam but Tan interrupted him as soon as he heard that his father had become involved with people smugglers.

'Cha (Father), the rest can wait. I will come and get you. Where did you say you were?'

'A little village called Nelson. I walked here from the fishing boat. I escaped and the men are looking for me.'

Tan suddenly started to panic but attempted to control the urge and think things through.

'The operator said it was near the South Australian border, south-western Victoria.'

He quickly tried to fathom how long it would take him to reach Nelson and estimated it would be approximately 300 kilometres. He looked at his watch.

'Cha, I have maps. I think I could get there in about three or four hours, depending on the terrain and the roads. There shouldn't be much traffic at this time of night. Where can I find you?'

'I am in a red telephone box in Nelson.'

'Which telephone box? There must be more than one?'

'Nelson is a very small village. There is only the one. It is outside a gas station.'

'Is there anywhere close you can hide until I get there?'

There was a pause and then his father said, 'There is a park or open ground with trees across the road. I could hide there.'

'Good,' said Tan. 'I will be driving a yellow pick-up. Wait for me.'

He gave Diem the registration number and added, 'Cha, be very careful. Make sure you keep out of sight and do not speak to anyone. Do you understand? No one.'

'I will take good care, my son.'

Tan hung up the phone, jumped out of bed, quickly threw on a pair of jeans and sweater, grabbed his wallet and went to exit but, having second thoughts, he returned, grabbed a blanket and the remains of his Vietnamese take-away banquet and fled to his ute, slamming the door of the flat after him.

*

Sally was sleeping soundly as Steve came out of the bathroom and headed for the kitchen for a glass of milk. He poured the cold liquid into a glass and sipped it as he wandered back through the lounge room, and noticed Sally's computer had been left on. He moved to switch it off and caught sight of the text Sally had been working on before his nightmare. Slowly he sat down and began to read. He tapped a couple of keys to bring the text back to the beginning and read the heading, 'The Continuing Adjustment of the Vietnam Veteran,' and the sub-heading that read, 'Combat-Related Post Trauma Stress Disorders.'

He looked towards the bedroom where Sally was sleeping, thoughts and doubts streaming through his mind, forcing him to confront the facts and wonder if this was the reason why she stayed with him? Did she really love him or was he nothing more than a guinea-pig for her academic advancement? He sat deep in thought for some time considering this disturbing and unexpected discovery. After finishing the document, he switched off the power to the machine and sat thinking for a long time.

Eventually he returned to bed. He lay, looking at Sally as she slept and feeling his closeness, she automatically cuddled up close to him, resting her arm across his body, her head touching his shoulder. The smell of her excited and comforted him.

Did it really matter? The most important thing was that he loved her like no one else he'd ever known and believed she loved him. What if she was using him? In his own way, wasn't he using her? Don't we all use each other in some way, he thought?

*

The dawn was just beginning to break as Tan's ute mounted a hill and he saw the little town of Nelson below. He'd made good time and driven mostly over the speed limit hoping not to be intercepted by a police patrol car. But the early morning hours and the rather remote location had been kind to him. Relieved and yet still anxious, he headed toward the town.

The sun was just peeping over the horizon as Tan entered the main, and what looked like the only, street in the little town. The early morning light was soft and filtered by the slight mist that was rising and dissipating into the clear sky above. He almost immediately saw the red phone box standing, as if on guard, outside the town's petrol station. The area was deserted at that hour and across the road from the phone box was the park that his father had described but there was no sign of the old man.

Tan parked, got out, and looking around, hurried to the phone box and wrenched open the door. It was obviously empty. Was this all a hoax? he asked himself: was the phone call from his father just a weird dream?

Slowly he turned back towards his ute and stopped. Diem was standing in the middle of the road wearing a crumpled suit and a long overcoat, and holding a battered suitcase in one hand. For a long time there was a stunned silence as the father and son stood looking at each other for the first time in more than ten years. Tears welled up in Diem's eyes as he made a tentative step toward his son and then stopped, unable to continue in the emotion of the moment. Tan also started to walk slowly towards his father and he too stopped a few paces away.

'Cha?' he managed to ask.

Hardly able to speak, choked with emotion, and almost unable to believe the miracle he was looking at, Diem whispered, '*Con trai?* ... Tan? (My son, Tan?)

For a long time both were lost for words standing facing each other awkwardly. Tan slowly realised that his father was alone and asked, 'Me?' (Mother?)

Diem could not answer but slowly pointed to the strip of white cloth hastily sewn onto the sleeve of his overcoat, which indicated mourning.

With tears beginning to roll down the cheeks of both father and son, Tan walked toward him and put his arms around his father in an emotional embrace, as the sun announced the first day of their new life together.

Chapter 9

Splicer stood waiting outside the locked garage office, slapping his arms and stomping his feet to warm himself as Steve's car drove in. Steve parked, got out and locked the car. He appeared a little distracted, still reflecting on his discovery of Sally's thesis and the implications.

'You're late,' Splicer said grumpily.

'Yeah, I know. I had to pick up the car.'

Noticing the plaster and bruises on Steve's face, he smirked.

'Oh ho, and what happened to you last night? Sally get stuck into you for overdoin' your quota?'

'Something like that,' Steve replied off-handedly, 'And how are you, Ken?'

'I'd be fine if someone would get this PC (Personnel Carrier) off me head.'

'Tie one on, did you?' Steve laughed.

'Nah, sober as a newt, I was. Probably the 'flu.'

Steve smiled and began the ritual of unlocking the garage and office, with Splicer in tow.

'Saw ya leave the pub with Sergeant Shithead last night. How would he be this mornin'?'

'On compo, I hope,' Steve replied.

'Good,' said Splicer. 'He'll starve to death waitin' for that.'

Steve moved towards the workshop, unlocked it and rolled open the doors with Splicer's help.

'Where's Tan?' asked Splicer.

Steve shrugged, a little annoyed. 'God knows. He was supposed to pick me up this morning and drive me over to get my car but he didn't show up.'

'That's not like Tan,' Splicer mused.

'No,' replied Steve, a little worried, 'No, it's not.'

Splicer was distracted by Steve's half-cabin cruiser, the *Long Tall Sally*, and her trailer parked in the workshop next to Su-Su.

'Had the boat out lately?'

'Not for weeks,' Steve replied, 'Might take her out at the weekend.'

Splicer turned his attention to his ailing truck. 'There you are, you slack bitch, bludging the night away in a nice warm garage.' He turned to Steve and whispered so Su-Su wouldn't overhear, 'How is she?'

'Give us a chance, we haven't had time to look at her yet,' Steve said a little aggravated.

'Shhhh,' Splicer hissed. 'Not so loud. When will ya know?'

Steve sighed. 'This afternoon. That is, if Tan ever shows up.'

Splicer placed his hand on Steve's arm and said almost pleadingly, 'There's a lot riding on her getting better, Steve.'

'Yeah, I know,' Steve relented, and then felt compelled to a give him some friendly advice. 'Look, Ken, I think you're flogging a dead horse, mate. Why don't you trade her in?'

As if he could, but he raised his voice so Su-Su could hear him, 'Yeah, well, I will one day.' And then he winked conspiratorially at Steve who sighed and turned away.

*

Sally, accompanied by Brenda, the receptionist, walked into Robert Heston's office. He stood behind his desk and greeted her warmly.

'Sally, darling …' He moved to her, kissed her on the cheek, and gave her a welcoming hug, which she accepted politely. 'How lovely to see you.'

'Hello, Robert.'

'Coffee?' he offered her.

'Thanks, but can't stay for long.'

Brenda nodded, and left. Sally sat in the visitor's chair.

There was a slightly awkward pause as Heston made his way back to his desk and sat.

'This is a surprise. I haven't seen you for weeks.'

'Yes, it has been quite a while, hasn't it? Sorry.'

'Well, how have you been? How's the thesis coming along?' he asked.

'Slowly,' she replied a little evasively. 'I'm actually thinking of dropping it – doing something else. But that's not what I came to see you about …'

'You can't be serious,' Robert interrupted, amazed, 'not after all the time and effort you've put into it.'

'It's very … awkward,' she replied, unable to meet his disapproving gaze.

'Of course it's awkward,' he agreed, 'but we've got a deal. That thesis will give you your Master's Degree. Think of the clinic … our clinic. I even supplied you with a class A guinea-pig.'

'Don't call him that!' she shot back sharply.

Heston took in her attitude and replied gently but objectively.

'He's a nice guy, Sally, and you've done wonders for him. But don't let it get out of hand. The two of you are hardly … equals.'

Heston would never understand how deep their relationship had become so she side-stepped the issue.

'You told him you didn't need to see him again for a month. Is he progressing that well?'

'From all the signs, yes he is. He still needs work, of course.'

Sally took a deep breath and approached the subject head on.

'He ran into an ex-sergeant from 'Nam last night and got into a bit of a fight with him.'

Heston looked at her levelly, reverting quickly to the therapist and waited, but she was finding it difficult to continue.

'How did he handle it?'

'On the surface, well, but ...' she paused uncertainly, 'it brought on that nightmare again, the one where he was wounded.'

Brenda knocked and entered with their coffee which she placed on the desk.

'Thanks, Brenda,' Heston said. 'That will be all.' Brenda exited with a smile at Sally.

He poured two cups of coffee, adding the sugar and milk as Sally liked it and took her cup over to her.

'That one has always had me puzzled a bit,' he said, back to business, 'Of course, it could've been the physical shock of being wounded but he's been able to equalize a lot of experiences as bad as that through the flooding treatment and counselling. I've noticed that a lot of his reactions are balancing out quite quickly now during the session as he's being more desensitised but there's always one particular sequence that stands out and the readings jump and he takes longer to recover.'

'And what sequence is that? Sally asked.

'Fire. Or to be more particular, anybody *on* fire,' he replied.

'He wasn't burnt,' Sally reminded him. 'He was hit by shrapnel. Maybe he's blocking something out, something he doesn't remember ... or won't let himself remember ... Something deeper.'

Heston nodded in agreement. 'Something that happened just before or just after he was wounded.'

Sally looked concerned. 'When he awoke after the nightmare, he couldn't remember details; he said he only had flashes and impressions of what happened. Everything appeared to be disjointed, he said; badly edited, like a film – nothing lineal.'

'I wonder if he'll ever let himself remember exactly what happened,' Robert mused.

*

Tan eventually arrived at the garage and entered the office. He was looking very tired from his long overnight haul and worries for his father, but Steve, who was sitting at his small, littered desk, working on some paperwork, at first didn't notice. He'd been so concerned about Tan's whereabouts, he automatically snapped at him in annoyed relief when Tan confronted him.

'Where the hell have you been? You were supposed to pick me up this morning. I had to get a bloody taxi to go and pick up my car.'

Tan was contrite.

'I'm sorry Steve. ... I ... I went around to some friend's place last night ... I had a bit too much to drink ... I fell asleep and ...'

'Great,' Steve replied, exasperated. 'I tried to ring you several times but you didn't answer.'

'I must've slept through it. Sorry.'

Steve sighed and relented, secretly relieved at discovering that Tan was alright. 'Well, if you feel up to it,' he said rather sarcastically, 'Splicer's truck has to be looked at and I have to get down to the bank.' He gathered up his paperwork, moved to the door and turned. 'Next time you get pissed and can't make it to work on time, give us a ring to let me know you're not dead on the road somewhere, will you?'

Tan nodded.

'In fact,' Steve added, 'give me a ring even if you *are* dead.' And with that he left the office and headed for his car.

Tan waited for Steve to drive off before he took a slip of paper out of his pocket, picked up the phone and dialled the number he had written down.

He waited for the number to answer and then said, 'Hello, Mr Wey?'

'Yes,' Wey answered.

'This is Nguyen Tan, a friend of Sally Grimes. She gave me your number some time back and I remember her saying if I or any of my friends needed advice, you were the man to talk to.'

'Well, I will try and do anything I can, Mr Nguyen,' Wey replied. 'How can I help?'

'Well, it is not something I can talk about on the phone. It concerns my parents.'

Reluctant to discuss any further details over the phone Tan asked Mr Wey if it was possible to make an appointment to meet privately. Mr Wey agreed and a time was set for eight o'clock that night.

*

In Melbourne's Little Collins Street, Captain Jonas, dressed impeccably and looking like a respectable businessman, walked into a modern, high-rise office block and went to the front reception desk. The receptionist greeted him and asked how she could help him. He told her his name was Geoffrey Browning and he had an appointment with a Mr Trench of Trench International Maritime. She checked her computer screen and directed him to the elevator and the twenty-ninth floor.

'Ah, yes, Mr Browning,' the secretary said. 'Mr Trench is expecting you. Would you like to follow me, please?'

She led him down a plush carpeted hallway to an office bearing the name Samuel Trench on a polished brass plate. She knocked and entered. Samuel Trench rose from behind his contemporary desk and moved around to greet his visitor with outstretched hand. He was a tall man, conservative in dress and manner with a deep cultured voice. He was in his late fifties and carried himself with natural authority. His greying hair was cut short and his eyes were a steely blue, set each side of a rather large nose with a slight hook.

'Geoffrey,' he smiled professionally, 'how good to see you. Sit down.' He gestured to the chair opposite his at the desk. 'Thank you, Miss Lang,' he said to his attractive, middle-aged secretary. 'That will be all.'

She exited, closing the door behind her.

Trench's friendly manner dropped immediately the door closed as he returned to his chair and sat looking coldly at Jonas.

'Why the hell did you have to bring me in here?' Jonas demanded.

Trench opened a drawer in his desk, removed a thick brown envelope and slid it across to Jonas. 'You could've sent the money by courier the way you usually do,' Jonas said as he reached over, picked up the envelope, opened it and quickly checked the contents.

'You were three down on this shipment,' Trench said icily. 'What happened?'

'It was unavoidable,' Jonas replied. 'Suspected typhoid. I didn't think we should take the risk. And it was two, not three.'

'Not according to the consignment delivery figures,' Trench said, removing a folder of papers from his desk drawer and referring to them. 'Tran Van Hoang, Nguyen Cuc ... and her husband, Nguyen Diem.'

'We had to dispose of the other two but old man Diem was there. I saw him on the trawler,' Jonas assured him.

'Well, he never arrived at the farm. According to the other refs, he never left the *Luger*.'

'Well, the bastards are covering up for him. I tell you I saw him board.'

Trench studied him steadily and then referred to another document.

'According to Bryce's report, Diem has a son living here. No address.'

Jonas stood and angrily paced the floor.

'The old bastard shot through! Probably when they were transferring to the trucks!' He jabbed a finger at Trench. 'Your boys cocked up. They're supposed to check. Did they search for him?'

'They did,' Trench shot back. 'There was no sign of him.'

'Shit!' said Jonas venomously.

Trench rose from his desk. 'I'll follow it through. If he hits town, we'll hear about it.'

But Jonas was obviously troubled, wondering if by then, it might be too late.

*

73

That night, Tan and Diem, trying to look as inconspicuous as possible, walked down a street in Melbourne's Chinatown, entered an old two-storey building and walked up the stairs to the second floor. They made their way down a dingy corridor until they came to a door marked 'China Imports', knocked and entered. Mr Wey rose to greet them and ushered them to chairs.

Although Tan and Diem were worried about exposing themselves in the open there seemed little option. Diem explained what had happened while Mr Wey listened attentively as he sat opposite them. When Diem had finished, Wey sat examining the information for a moment. He shook his head in disbelief.

'This is incredible. One hears rumours from time to time about such organisations as this, but I never thought they held much substance.'

'So you have not encountered anyone who has had dealings with these people?' Tan asked.

Wey shook his head. 'No, but that is not surprising. From what you say, they are obviously a large and powerful concern who would control their people by fear of deportation.'

'Or death,' Tan added ominously. 'Officially, these illegals do not exist and can be disposed of with little fear of retribution.'

Wey rose and walked to look out the grimy window and then turned to Diem, 'You are certain your wife was murdered, Mr Diem?'

'Yes,' Diem replied. 'I saw the marks around her throat. There could be no mistake.'

'My father concealed his knowledge from them as he knew they would kill him too if they thought he suspected.'

'There was another man supposedly left on board who I think was also murdered,' Diem added.

'And what was to happen to the others?' Wey asked.

'They were to be split up and sent to work on farms, growing dope we suspected, and processing laboratories. A couple of people on board had previous experience in that field.'

'They were only escaping one form of slavery for another,' Tan concluded bitterly. 'My father believes he must expose this organisation to the authorities, even at the cost of his own safety. But I thought you may be able to suggest some other way without involving him directly.'

Wey gestured helplessly. 'I wish I could but I am only an ordinary businessman. This matter is not within my range. I can only suggest you go directly to the Commonwealth Police or the Immigration Department ...'

Suddenly another possible solution occurred to him. 'Just a moment.' He went to his filing cabinet and started searching. 'Not long ago I had dealings with an investigator from the Immigration Department.' He found the file he was looking for. 'Yes, here it is – a Mr Lyons. Actually he was very helpful ... I could approach him – unofficially – and see what he suggests.'

Tan and Diem looked more hopeful. 'You would not have to mention my father's name, or where he is?'

Wey returned to his desk with the file. 'Not at this stage, no.'

Greatly relieved, Tan shook Wey's hand.

'Thank you, Mr Wey, I cannot tell you how ...'

But Wey held up his hands, interrupting him. 'I can promise you nothing at this stage.'

'I know,' Tan assured him.

'But we must try. Your father has been through enough already and we must protect others who may fall into the same trap.'

Tan nodded as Wey continued.

'You must go very carefully. Talk to no one else until you hear from me. These people will know by now your father has escaped and no doubt they will have many informers on the lookout for him.' He turned to Tan, 'Leave me your telephone number where I can contact you.'

Tan was automatically reticent about giving out any information that may allow them to be traced.

'No, I will ring you tomorrow if you don't mind, and see if you have come up with anything.'

'As you wish,' Wey said, 'but remember – do nothing and keep well out of sight until we speak further.'

Tan and Diem shared a worried look and stood, thanked Mr Wey for his help, and rose to leave.

As they left the building, there were quite a few people in the street, heading home from work or planning to dine at the many restaurants in the area. All of them looked suspicious to Tan and Diem but no one seemed to be taking any particular notice of just another two Asians in Chinatown. They walked back to Tan's ute, got in and drove off.

What they had not noticed was a Chinese street photographer in his early forties, carrying a camera and watching them from a concealed position in a doorway. His name was Yin Foo and as he watched Tan and Diem depart he took a mental note of the ute's registration number, jotted it down in a notebook and hurried across the street to a nearby phone booth.

As Tan drove his father back home, Diem was hesitant about involving Mr Wey in his dangerous situation.

'How did you know of this Mr Wey?' he asked.

'I told you. He is well respected for the work he does for the Asian community,' his son replied. 'His photograph is often in the newspapers. My friend Sally has often spoken highly of him.'

Diem frowned, not thoroughly convinced, expressing his age-old mistrust.

'He is Chinese.'

Tan smiled. 'Does it matter? We're in Australia now.'

Diem looked at him as if he were joking.

'We are hardly in a position to choose, Cha,' Tan said.

Out in the suburbs, Tan pulled into the kerb across the street from his favourite Vietnamese restaurant, Saigon Sam's.

'Why are we stopping?' Diem asked, alarmed.

'We are going to celebrate your arrival. I am taking you to dinner,' Tan said as he engaged the handbrake.

'You have been away too long, *con trai*. We are in mourning for one year. We cannot celebrate.'

Tan sighed patiently. 'Very well, we will not celebrate, but we must eat. I am starving.'

'Your Mr Wey said we should stay out of sight.'

'Sam's place is perfectly safe,' Tan assured him. 'He is a friend. Steve, Sally and I eat here a lot.'

Diem was not entirely convinced but they got out of the ute and entered the fairly crowded but unpretentious restaurant. Sam, the proprietor, was busy serving at the other end of the room. Tan caught his eye and waved. Sam waved back and indicated a table by the front window that was just becoming vacant. Tan guided his father to it and they sat. Diem covertly studied the other diners looking for possible enemies. There appeared to be a mixture of nationalities, but mainly Asian, eating and chatting happily. Tan had to raise his voice to be heard above the din.

'Sam's real name is Than Van Minh. He has been here for many years. He named the place after the bar he ran for the GIs in Saigon. He thought he was immigrating to America but he finished up here.'

Sam made his way over to their table, beaming happily and displaying a wonderful set of white teeth that featured one gold front tooth which sparkled in the light from the traditional Vietnamese lamps that illuminated the restaurant.

He greeted them profusely in an outlandishly strong American accent.

'Heeey, baby,' he shouted at Tan. 'Give me five, man, long time no see!'

Tan stood and laughingly gave him a high five. 'Hello, Sam, I'd like you to meet my friend, Diem … Nhat Diem. He has only recently arrived.'

'How's it goin', Mr Nhat? Welcome to the land of the free. Well, not the real land of the free but it'll do for the time being. Just got out, eh? Well, what d'ya know. How was the trip out, a pain in the ass, I'll bet?'

Before the stunned Diem could answer, Sam ploughed on.

'Just wait till you settle in, bro, you'll get to love it.' He chuckled happily. 'Sure beats the crap outta those refugee camps, I can tell you.'

'Mr Nhat was sponsored by his family. He didn't have to stay in the refugee camps. Now, what's on the menu tonight?' Tan said, trying to divert any further attention away from his father. 'Busy night, Sam?'

'Yeah, man, the place has been jumpin' since early. Where's Steve and Sally?'

'Ah,' replied Tan evasively, 'they could not make it tonight but they send their regards.'

'Pity,' Sam responded. 'Nice couple – especially her. She's a doll. Okay, what'll it be, gents?'

Tan was amused as he handed Diem the menu. The old man was sitting in open-mouthed shock at this larger-than-life character.

*

In another bistro closer to home, Sally and Steve were also dining, and Steve was discussing Tan's unfathomable behaviour that day.

'It's not just that, he's got something on his mind,' he said to Sally. 'He's been vague all day.'

'Maybe he's got money problems,' Sally offered. 'He tries to send as much back to his family as he can.'

'He sent them a thousand a few weeks back through the black market.'

'I wonder how much of that the family got,' Sally replied cynically.

Steve shrugged. 'Six hundred, maybe?'

'Well, that's probably better than they would've done through the official channels.' Another possibility came to mind. 'Maybe he's got another girlfriend?'

Steve shook his head. 'He would've told me.'

Sally smiled. 'He might just want to check her out for himself this time before he gets your approval.'

Steve smiled sweetly at her inference. 'Very funny.'

'Maybe it's unrequited love?'

'What's that?'

'He wants it but he ain't getting it.'

'You know,' Steve replied, 'for a high class dame you've got a very coarse turn of phrase.'

'I'm the product of my current environment,' Sally conceded.

Steve suddenly recalled the secret thesis Sally was writing and asked, 'Didn't they warn you that's one of the side-effects of slumming?'

Something in his manner made her feel a little uncomfortable, and she replied seriously, 'I don't consider I'm *slumming* ... Do you?'

'Well, you've got to admit, you're a rich, educated sheila from the other side of the tracks,' he replied lightly. 'And you've got looks to die for. And I'm just a boring, loony slob who runs a garage. What do you see in me?'

'Sex and the body of a Greek god,' she replied equally lightly. 'Do you think I want you for your mind?'

She stared into his eyes. 'Apart from that,' she said more seriously, 'I happen to love you.'

He was starting to feel embarrassed about trying to catch her out and decided not to continue along that line.

'Forget it,' he said, trying to keep up his former playfulness. 'My body's not up for sale – or my mind.'

And then changing back to the original subject he said brightly, 'Listen, about Tan, maybe we should call around after we've eaten and drag it out of him?'

Sally responded with one of her familiar warning looks.

'Steve ...'

He quickly reconsidered. 'Alright, alright, I know, he's a big boy now and he wants to look after himself.'

Sally nodded in agreement, but Steve continued to speculate.

As Tan and Diem sat eating their meal two rough-looking youths wearing jeans and hooded jackets entered and stood looking around the restaurant. Tan was too busy eating to notice at first. A couple sitting at the next table, having finished their meal, stood, and leaving the money for their bill on the table, departed. The two young men moved to the now vacant table and sat down. One of them picked up the money and stuffed it in his pocket, but Sam noticed and approached the table angrily.

'Hey, I saw that, buddy. Come on, hand it over.'

The youth looked up defiantly. 'What are ya talkin' about, chinkie?'

'The money those people left for their bill, wise guy. I didn't come in on the last boat, y'know,' Sam said dangerously.

The two louts sneered at each other, and the apparent leader said, 'What money, slope eyes? They didn't leave no money.'

'Nah,' his mate agreed, 'they must've skipped through without payin', slopie. You can't trust no one now days.'

By now Tan and Diem were alerted to the argument and Tan made ready to intervene if Sam needed help. Sam had had enough and grabbed one of the louts roughly by the jacket front and dragged him to his feet.

'Alright, you punks, that's it. Hand it over or I call the cops.'

Suddenly the other hoon erupted and pushed Sam and his mate violently, smashing them into Tan and Diem's table, sending food and crockery flying. Tan was quick to respond and jumped to his feet to retaliate and a brawl developed. Some of the women patrons screamed and their menfolk yelled and joined in the fray and pretty soon havoc reigned with tables and chairs being knocked over, food and drinks flying through the air, punches being thrown and bodies crashing. Diem cowered in a corner, terrified.

At the height of the commotion, one of the louts kept Sam and Tan occupied while the other one pulled a knife and manoeuvred his way over to Diem who by now had been thrown to the floor and sat cringing in a corner. The old man shrank back in shock, trying to protect himself with his hands. Just as the young crim was about to sink the knife into Diem, Tan suddenly saw what was happening and threw himself across the room, grabbed the would-be assailant and sent him crashing against the wall. The second lout threw himself at Diem but could not get to him as Tan was protecting his father fiercely.

By then a couple of the male patrons had started to get things under control and pretty soon the louts were coming off second best. Realising they were outnumbered, the hooligans escaped out into the street and ran for their car. Sam tried to follow but they were too quick for him and roared off.

Sam cursed and returned to the restaurant. With hands on hips, he surveyed the wreckage and was mystified.

'This is crazy, man,' he said to Tan. 'We've never had no trouble like this before.' He turned to the other patrons and said, 'Sorry, everybody. Anybody hurt?' He then moved around the room trying to comfort the disturbed diners.

Tan helped his still shaking father to his feet.

'Are you alright?'

Diem was still in shocked disbelief.

'He tried to knife me,' he said aghast.

By now, Tan had started putting two and two together.

'Yes,' he said, confirming Diem's suspicions.

'Why would he do that?' the old man asked. 'You said we would be safe here.'

But suddenly they heard the sound of a police siren in the distance, coming closer.

'We had better go,' Tan said, as he threw some money on the table for the bill, and taking his father by the arm, led him to the door.

They left the restaurant and stepped off the curb to cross the street, heading for Tan's ute. They were almost in the middle of the road when suddenly an old hotted-up sedan, driven by the two louts, screamed out from the curb and headed straight for them. Tan grabbed his father, pushed him toward the ute and out of the path of the oncoming sedan then immediately threw himself out of harm's way. The sedan roared by narrowly missing both of them and then, with screeching brakes, the driver stopped and attempted to throw his car into a U-turn. Tan desperately scrambled to his feet, yelling to his father to get into the ute.

Diem flung open the passenger door and threw himself in, closely followed by Tan, jumping into the driver's seat. He started the ignition, the motor caught, and he swerved out into the road. The sedan completed its three-point turn and roared after them in hot pursuit.

The two vehicles, with Tan's ute in the lead, sped through the back streets in a frantic chase. It had begun to rain making the roads slippery and dangerous but Tan managed to hold the road and even increase their lead, with both cars sliding into and out of corners at reckless speed.

In the sedan, Wes, the driver was furious as he realised they were falling behind their prey.

'Rotten chink bastard! That ute's souped up!' he screamed.

His mate Donny, in the passenger seat, was starting to get a bit worried at Wes's hairy driving.

'Give it away, Wes, we don't have a chance now,' he urged.

Wes swerved violently to avoid an on-coming car which caused Donny to yell, 'Jeeeeesus! You've been watchin' too much fuckin' telly! The only way we'll catch 'em now is if they run out of fuckin' petrol!'

But Wes hadn't thought that far in advance.

'Shut the fuck up!' he yelled back.

They came to an intersection just as the traffic lights were about to turn red and Tan shot through. By the time the sedan hit the intersection the lights were against them but they ploughed through regardless. They failed to notice a police patrol car on duty parked just around the corner. With lights flashing and siren blaring, the police car gave chase. The officer driving called in the traffic violation and their position and asked for back-up to intercept the speeding sedan.

Tan drove on using as many detours and tricks as he could to out-run the pursuing sedan. He checked the rear view mirror and smiled.

'I think we've lost them, Cha.'

But Diem didn't feel entirely convinced. They happened to pass the bistro where Sally and Steve had been dining and were just preparing to leave. They just missed seeing Tan and his father speed past as they arrived outside, and as they made to cross the street to Steve's car the hoons' sedan rounded the corner and roared towards them. Steve roughly pushed Sally back onto the kerb out of the path of the oncoming car. The sedan flashed past but just at that instant, the back-up police car arrived at a right angle out of a side street and swung a sharp left-hand turn to intercept the sedan. There was a horrendous screeching of brakes followed by a loud crash as the sedan swerved violently and side-swiped the patrol car, sending it skidding across the road and rolling over onto its hood. The sedan, out of control, ricocheted across the road and smashed into a parked house painter's van loaded with paint and solvent.

There was a horrific explosion and Donnie, not wearing a seatbelt, was catapulted from the car, landing in a mangled heap on the road. The liquid flames shot into the air and onto the sedan, setting it and occupant alight. The young driver, Wes, with clothes blazing, flung himself out of the car, scrambled to his feet, screaming in pain and terror. With arms outstretched and engulfed in flames, he stumbled towards the mesmerised Steve.

Steve's nightmare suddenly became vividly alive as, once again, he saw the burning Vietnamese boy stumbling towards him. His face contorted in horror, he tried to back away but the memory held him firmly in its grasp and paralysed him. Suddenly he covered his face with his hands, screamed and threw himself to the ground. 'Grenade!'

Automatically jarred into action by the accident, Sally had immediately run to the upturned police car to check on the condition of the two officers. Finding they were both conscious, she turned her attention to the blazing lout and quickly threw her overcoat over him to douse the flames and yelled at the bystanders who had rushed out of the bistro.

'Call an ambulance and the fire brigade – quickly!'

It was then she heard the familiar scream and looked back to see Steve, writhing on the ground, obviously injured.

'Steve!' she screamed in panic as she ran to him.

She fell to her knees beside him. There was no sign of injury but he was babbling and shaking violently. She took him in her arms and he desperately clung to her.

'Gre ... gren ... grenade!' he screamed again.

Shocked by his unexpected, terrified outburst and his obvious relapse, she held him tightly, rocking him gently and trying to soothe him.

The ambulance arrived, attended to the police officers and the wounded sedan drivers and took them to hospital with siren blaring. They wanted to take Steve with them but Sally explained that he wasn't physically hurt but in shock which, as his trained nurse and carer, she would attend to at home. They didn't have time to argue with her as they wanted to get the injured to hospital as soon as they could. But they advised her to get him to a hospital as quickly as possible. Steve had gone suddenly silent but was still shaking uncontrollably as a couple of bystanders helped Sally get him into the car. She ran to the driver's side, threw herself into the front seat and headed for home.

Chapter 10

Tan and Diem drove on, unaware of the carnage in their wake as they were out of sight when it happened. Tan constantly checked the rear-view mirror for any signs of pursuit.

'Looks like we have lost them,' he said to his father.

Diem was only too aware that the danger had not passed.

'They will find me again,' he said with quiet conviction.

He paused, considering his limited options.

'I do not think we can wait for your Mr Wey. I will go to the authorities tomorrow.'

Concerned for his father's safety and the risk involved of possible deportation by going to the authorities, Tan frowned.

'We'll talk about it when we get home.'

*

Sally had medicated Steve and put him to bed when they'd returned to the house. She stood in the bedroom doorway and watched him. He was now sleeping but she crept to the bedside table and took the bottle of sleeping pills away and hid them on a top shelf in the kitchen. She then moved to the phone in the living room and dialled Robert Heston's number but her call went straight to his answering service so she hung up. She decided she needed a drink and moved to the drinks cabinet, unlocked it and poured herself a large Scotch. She took her drink to the outside deck and sat, deep in thought, the pale moonlight illuminating the concern on her face.

In the bedroom Steve had slipped into a deep sleep and his eyelids began to flicker as the nightmare slithered from his subconscious like a deadly snake and once again took control of his mind. The night's events had activated the deep-seated memory again. But this time it wasn't as disjointed as it had been previously and it seemed to play out in a continuous stream of mind film. For the first time ever there was an order in the details of events as he relived them.

Once again he saw it as if through the lens of his camera, as if he were filming the scenes, which of course, he had been. He'd believed that by filming the traumatic events he encountered he was somewhat removed from the reality and it didn't seem to affect him as drastically. He'd become mesmerised by his work and the immediacy of the moment.

But it did affect him, as seeing a horror film could sometimes spark a nightmare in a child long after the initial viewing.

In his mind he heard once again the soundtrack of the jungle. But he could smell the odours and he could feel the sweat misting his body and trickling down his back and armpits. His lens panned across the thick jungle, the shafts of bright sunlight that streamed through the canopy above, the patches of threatening shadows. He saw close-ups of the strained and camouflaged faces of Finch, Splicer and Joey and others of the platoon as they crept silently along a jungle path. Ricketts was leading but his expression was different. His cruel face tense but excited, his eyes ever watchful against ambush.

As in a film, the scene cut to a small clearing. The soldiers squatted behind the underbrush watching the activity. In the middle of the clearing there was a group of rough huts. Women dressed in traditional *ao canh*, white loose tops hanging over baggy black trousers, and wearing *non la*, the conical straw hat, sat at open fires cooking. A few children played listlessly, laughing and talking occasionally. The men, also dressed in the wide-bottomed, baggy black trousers that allowed them to be rolled up in the water of the rice fields, and black long sleeved tops, sat about in groups chatting and smoking. They were always smoking. Vietnamese were the heaviest smokers in the world.

A few were cleaning automatic rifles.

Ricketts gave a hand signal to his men and all hell broke loose.

They stormed the clearing, screaming, with weapons blazing. The air was suddenly filled with smoke and the cacophony of grenade explosions and gunfire. Peasants scattered for cover and their weapons. Women and children screamed in terror as they ran and fell. The scene cut to a grinning Ricketts, shooting one of the men in the stomach, the guts being ripped from his body and blood spurting and splattering on the ground, then panning to a woman nearby, cowering and desperately crawling towards a rifle. Ricketts kicked the weapon away, raised his bayonet and sank it into her throat. Three small children, running for the surrounding jungle, were cut down by machine gun fire: a montage of horror of people screaming and killing and being killed.

Steve relived the bile rising in his throat as the 'film' became edited in his mind: Joey's arm flying off his body and spinning in the air before it hit the ground. He heard his own desperate scream for 'Medic!' Ricketts running into a shack and blasting a man and woman with withering fire, the blood spattering their young son cringing nearby, the boy screaming in terror and running for the entrance; Ricketts grabbing a flaming brand of wood, running after the lad and setting his clothes on fire, the boy becoming a hideous flaming torch.

In Steve's mind, the lens disappeared and he saw the scene in shocking reality. He'd dropped the camera which now hung from his shoulder by the strap, and was staring in horrified disbelief. Suddenly he was overwhelmed by the senseless killing, the slaughter of innocent children, the butchery of people who just wanted to run their own country free from colonialism. He ran to the boy, desperately trying to save him by knocking him to the ground and trying to smother the flames that were engulfing the young, waif-like body. He turned and yelled to his journalist mate, Stan, calling out for him to help.

But behind Stan he saw Ricketts holding a primed grenade in his hand. Appalled and in horrified disbelief, he watched Ricketts, as if in slow motion, carefully lob the grenade in their direction and quickly duck behind the covering wall of the shack. In desperation Steve screamed, 'Grenade!' and dived for an indentation in the ground caused by a mortar shell. He heard again the deafening explosion as the grenade detonated. He felt again the pain in his back, hip, shoulder and leg as the shrapnel tore into his body. And as the smoke, flames and dust settled, through the pain and the blackness creeping in on his vision, he saw the burning body of the young boy he had tried to save and his journalist mate, Stan, mutilated by the grenade explosion. Then Ricketts' boots, close to his face, came into his fading view. A boot crashed down, smashing his camera and the precious tapes that had fallen from Steve's pack.

He screamed again.

'Nooooo!'

He woke instantly, sitting bolt upright in the bed, his body trembling and bathed in sweat. His mind was suddenly terribly clear and alive as he recalled, for the first time, the total facts of the experience that previously his memory had refused to reveal to his consciousness. Still breathing heavily from the nightmare, he eventually sank back onto the pillows and moaned, 'Jesus ...'

Hearing his scream, Sally came running and again stopped in the doorway, staring at him anxiously. But this time he appeared somehow different: calmer, almost in control.

'Steve?' she said apprehensively.

He looked at her for a long time before he finally said,

'Suoi Luc ... The patrol ... I remember! I remember what happened ... I remember it all ...'

She went over and sat on the bed next to him and took his hand.

Slowly and unemotionally, as if in a long-forgotten memory, he began to recount the whole story as she sat and listened, growing more horrified by the minute.

*

The next morning, Tan was getting ready to leave for work while Diem sat at the kitchen table drinking his coffee. They had been discussing the implications of the previous night's events and Tan looked anxious.

'Just one more day, Cha,' he said, 'until I talk to Mr Wey. If he has not been able to arrange anything with his contact, we will go to the authorities.'

Diem looked at him doubtfully and Tan added, 'I give you my word.'

He picked up his work bag and moved to the door.

'I will ring you when I hear from him.'

At the door he turned. 'Lock the door after me … and don't let anyone in, and I mean *anyone*.'

Diem nodded and rose to lock the door behind his son.

*

Sally awoke early and was surprised to find Steve not in bed beside her. She heard the shower running, got out of bed, pulled on a robe and headed for the bathroom and was astounded to find Steve, showering. She pulled back the shower curtain.

'Well, good morning.'

'Morning,' he replied, as he finished showering and turned off the water.

'And what do you think you're doing?'

'Three guesses. Could you pour the coffee and shove on some toast? I'm running late.'

Sally was amazed that after the previous night's experience he appeared almost back to normal.

'You're not going to work?' she said incredulously.

'I've got to. We're flat out,' he replied as he grabbed a towel and started drying himself briskly.

'After last night?' she enquired disbelievingly.

'I'm alright,' he reassured her. 'Honest.'

Sally looked very doubtful but sighed resignedly.

'Well, promise me you'll call in and see Rob Heston, or at least, ring him. You should talk to him about the nightmare.'

He finished drying himself, threw the towel in the basket and took her in his arms.

'Sally, I have to handle this myself – and I will.'

He held her away from him and looked in her eyes. He could see that she was genuinely concerned and consoled her.

'Alright, I'll ring Rob – if I get time.'

She nodded dubiously, knowing that would be very unlikely, and surrendered.

'You know I'll agree to anything when you're naked and look at me like that,' she said and slapped him lightly on the bum.

Steve worked on a Mercedes which was up on the hoist while, alongside, Tan worked under Splicer's truck, Su-Su, which was up on manual jacks. Beside Tan, under the truck were a large, heavy metal tool box and a work light on a steel stand about thirty centimetres high. Not wanting to upset Tan, Steve had not mentioned last night's events and had been subtly trying to pump Tan on his whereabouts.

'So, it was a good night, eh?'

'Yes,' Tan said noncommittally, as he attempted to loosen the oil plug with a spanner.

There was a pause before Steve said, 'Where did you say you went again?'

'I didn't,' Tan said as he slid out from under the truck. 'I met a friend and we went out to dinner.' He slid back under the truck.

'Oh, yeah,' Steve said pretending to recall. 'She must be pretty special … I mean, you usually eat out with us on Tuesdays. You could've brought her along. Ashamed of us, eh?'

'Yes,' Tan replied caustically, 'especially when you pry.'

'I wasn't prying, mate, I was just ...' But he was interrupted by the phone ringing in the office.

'I'll get it,' he said as he climbed out of the pit, wiped his hands on an oil rag, and headed for the office.

'Steve's Garage,' he said into the mouthpiece. 'Who? ... Yeah, I see ... Well, I will if I can. What's the problem?'

The caller was obviously going to a lot trouble trying to explain his predicament and Steve listened patiently. A solid-looking man dressed in a black, pin-striped suit entered the office and stood waiting for Steve to finish his call. Steve placed his hand over the mouthpiece and said to the stranger, 'Won't be a minute.'

The stranger nodded and turned to face the window which overlooked the entrance to the garage. A dark sedan had pulled up outside the service bay and two men, also wearing suits, got out, looked around to check they were not being watched and entered the service bay where Tan was working.

Engrossed in his work, Tan was not aware of the two men entering. They paused for a moment and then one of them walked over to the manual jack that was holding the truck up for Tan to work under. Suddenly, with a crash, the jack was snap-released and the truck came crashing down on Tan. He screamed and the two men disappeared out the entrance, jumped into their car and sped off.

Steve heard the crash and slammed down the phone in shock.

'Jesus – Tan!' he yelled as he fled from the office towards the service bay. The stranger hurried out after him, quickly got into his car and drove off. In a panic, Steve saw that the jack had slipped and only Tan's legs could be seen sticking out from under Su-Su.

'Tan!' he yelled, 'My God – Tan!'

'I'm alright,' Tan's voice replied shakily. 'The toolbox and light saved me ... But I can't move ... Jack it up ... Quickly!

Steve raced to the jack, engaged the arm and raised the truck. He then grabbed Tan's feet and gently pulled him out.

'What happened?' he asked in astonishment.

'The release catch must've slipped,' Tan said.

'Fuck,' said Steve, 'you were lucky you weren't killed!'

'Yes,' agreed Tan, still shaken.

Steve helped him to his feet, put his arm around Tan's shoulders and helped him back towards the office. He then went to the filing cabinet, opened the bottom drawer and extracted a brandy bottle and a couple of glasses, set them on the desk and poured two slugs into the glasses.

'Didn't you have the safety pin in?'

'I thought I did,' replied Tan.

Steve handed one of the glasses to Tan.

'Well, for Christ's sake, don't go back under until I check it out.'

Tan nodded and gratefully took the brandy, swallowing it down in one gulp.

Steve downed his drink and immediately went to pour himself another but checking himself from falling into that trap, screwed the lid back on the bottle and replaced it in the filing cabinet drawer. Only then did he notice that the stranger who had appeared in the office only minutes earlier was no longer to be seen.

'Jesus, some people,' he said in disgust.

'What?' replied Tan.

'There was a bloke here waiting to see me. I was tied up with some cretin on the phone when I heard the crash. He didn't even come and see if he could help, did he? He just pissed off!'

Tan suddenly began to suspect that the jack may not have been faulty and the truck falling on him may not have been an accident after all.

*

In her office, Sally was on the phone to Robert Heston. She asked him if Steve had called or been in to see him yet. From his answer it was obvious, although not surprising, that Steve had not contacted Robert as he said he would.

'Oh, I see,' she said into the phone. 'Yes, I know but something happened last night and I think you should know about it, for Steve's sake … No, I don't want to explain it over the phone. Can I meet you somewhere?'

Robert invited her to his office to talk it over but she declined saying she'd better not in case Steve did turn up while she was there. He understood and offered to meet her in the park opposite his building.

'Yes, that would be fine,' she said, 'when?' She checked her watch and said, 'Right, I'll see you then. Thanks, Robert.'

She hung up feeling guilty about going behind Steve's back, but nevertheless, she rose from her desk, picked up her handbag and hurried from the office.

*

Back in the garage workshop, Steve checked the jack that had apparently failed when Tan was underneath Splicer's truck but was puzzled to find nothing obviously wrong with it. He stood for a few moments trying to work out the cause of the accident and with no immediate solution coming to mind, he wandered back to the office where he had left Tan. But as he approached the open door he overheard Tan on the phone and stopped to listen.

'No,' Tan was saying, 'I am sorry but I cannot agree to that … Yes, I know, but that was last night. A lot has happened since then and I will not take the risk … No, we will meet you and your contact in the lounge of the Royal Hotel at eight o'clock. There will be a lot of people around and there is a police station a few doors away. If we are not satisfied we will go straight to the police and take our chances.'

Steve stepped into the office and stood looking at Tan, who hurriedly finished the conversation.

'I must go now. I will see you tonight? … Thank you.'

Tan hung up and looked at Steve guiltily.

'Don't you think it's time you let me in on what's going on?' Steve asked softly.

'I cannot get you involved,' Tan replied, not able to meet Steve's eyes.

'Don't be bloody stupid,' Steve pressed him. 'I thought we were mates – more than mates.'

Tan shook his head and moved to pass Steve at the door but Steve held his arm, preventing Tan from dismissing him.

'We are mates,' Tan said, 'but this is my responsibility and I must handle it.' He turned back to Steve as his arm was reluctantly released.

'I will be able to tell you tomorrow,' he said and then made his way back to the workshop.

Steve sighed, wounded that Tan was excluding him and his offer of help.

*

Sally and Robert Heston strolled through the park as she told him of Steve's reaction to the previous night's events and the subsequent nightmare.

Sally was obviously still emotionally concerned but Robert, always the psychologist, was almost jubilant.

'So that was it? Yes!' He slapped one fist into the palm of his other hand. 'That would explain the slight inconsistency in his reactions during the flooding programme!'

'How do you mean?' Sally asked. 'I thought you said he was responding normally.'

'Almost, but not quite,' Robert answered. 'I thought he must've been giving me a reaction to fire, but it didn't always show up.'

Sally looked at him in puzzlement.

'Don't you see, it wasn't *fire* he was reacting to, it was seeing someone *on* fire … The young driver on fire. The boy in his nightmare! That's what he was suppressing. His mind had never let him recall that before. The boy on fire! The burning boy! That was the key. That's what unlocked the memory.'

Robert was completely involved in the clinical aspect of the case while Sally was more worried about Steve on a more personal level.

'And you said he acted quite normally this morning?' Heston continued.

'As far as I could tell,' Sally replied, 'but it's not that easy to be sure with Steve. He tends to cover things up.'

'And he remembered everything from last night? The accident, the nightmare, every detail?' he persisted.

'He seemed to.'

'Good, good. It looks like he's examining it and trying to get it into perspective.'

'But why didn't he come to see you?'

Robert grinned. 'He's trying not to depend on me. He wants to work it out for himself.'

'And if he can't,' Sally asked, dubiously.

'*Then* he'll come to me,' he replied confidently. 'It depends on just how strong he's become.'

'But it could send him back into a relapse if he's not as strong as you think?'

'Yes, we can never tell. In the wrong circumstances …' he paused, considering the situation before he said, 'He's come a long way back. I wonder if it's far enough.'
He turned to her with a smile. 'Interesting bit for your thesis.'

But Sally's mind was more on the man she loved than the clinical, psychological implications.

*

That evening, Steve's car cruised to a stop across the road, a short distance from the Royal Hotel which Steve had heard Tan mention on the phone. From their position, Steve and Sally had a clear view of the entrance. He had explained to her his concern about what he'd overheard of Tan's telephone conversation but she was very unsure they were doing the right thing by interfering.

'Alright,' she said, 'so what do we do now?'

'We wait,' Steve said uneasily.

'For what?'

'I don't know,' he said in exasperation.

'Don't you think you might be overreacting a bit?' she said gently.

'No, I don't think I am,' he snapped, almost brusquely.

'Look,' she tried to reason with him, 'you two have a very special relationship. You're closer than brothers. Don't you think he'd tell you if he needed your help?'

'All I know,' he replied, 'is that he's involved in some sort of danger. Otherwise why would he talk about going to the police?'

'I don't know,' she sighed helplessly, 'but it may be something ...'

But she was interrupted suddenly by noticing Mr Wey and a younger Caucasian man walking out of the car park and heading for the hotel entrance.

'Oh,' she said in surprise, 'there's Mr Wey.'

'Who's he?' Steve asked.

'Just a man I know through work,' she replied. Was this some sort of coincidence or was there some connection with Tan's problem? After all, Mr Wey had a record of helping Asian migrants.

'Who's the guy with him?' Steve asked, wondering if the two men could be possibly linked to Tan's secret assignation, but Sally shook her head.

'I don't know.'

Steve suddenly saw Tan and an old man crossing the road a short distance up from them also heading for the hotel entrance.

'There he is,' whispered Steve. 'Who's the old guy with him, I wonder?'

They watched as Tan stopped outside the hotel, looked around casually and seeing nothing suspicious, entered the hotel with Diem.

'I feel like we're spying on him,' Sally muttered uncomfortably.

'You think I'm enjoying it?' snapped Steve.

Overcoming his guilt, he turned back to watch the hotel.

Alone and unnoticed by Wey and his companion, Glen Lyons, Tan observed the two men as they settled themselves at a table in the lounge area of the hotel. His eyes travelled around the room, checking it out for any possible trap. Seeing nothing untoward, he walked across as inconspicuously as he could and stood by their table. Wey looked up, stood and greeted him warmly.

'Ah, Mr Tan, I'm so glad you could make it.' They shook hands and Wey introduced Lyons. 'This is Mr Lyons, the gentleman I spoke to you about.' Wey looked around the room and said to Tan, 'But where is your father?'

'He will be along presently,' Tan replied and turned to Lyons. 'Excuse me for asking, Mr Lyons, but do you have any identification?'

'Of course.' Lyons produced his wallet from his inside coat pocket and offered his ID.

Tan read it aloud. 'A special Investigator for the Department of Immigration and Ethnic Affairs.'

'You're perfectly at liberty to check it out of course. In fact I think you should,' Lyons reassured him.

Tan studied the ID carefully and handed it back. 'Thank you.'

'Let us sit,' said Wey.

'And what assistance can you offer my father, Mr Lyons?' Tan asked quietly.

'Protection and legal immigrant status,' Lyons said, 'in return for information.'

Tan studied the man's handsome face to catch any sign of trickery, but at the same time, daring to hope he could be the answer to his father's problem.

Lyons looked around the room to see if anyone was eavesdropping and reassured, spoke quietly and confidentially.

'Mr Tan, for some time now the Department has had its suspicions that an operation, such as your father described to Mr Wey here, exists. It would have to be a very large and sophisticated organisation with extensive financial backing, probably Asian in origin. But our investigations have all led to a dead end, in some cases I don't mean that figuratively. Over the past twelve months, three unidentified bodies have been washed ashore along the coast. All three were Asian and none were carrying identification papers and none looked like local fishermen. We have spies planted in the Asian community but as yet, nothing has come to light, only vague rumours. It's a very tight community as I am sure you will agree and we need evidence.' He paused to let it sink in. 'Now, can I see your father?'

Tan digested the information, realising his father could be the key to unlocking a vast illegal operation, preying on the fears and weaknesses of people who were desperate to escape from the suffering and tyranny of their own countries. However, what would be the cost? What would be the danger involved? How could he know unless he was prepared to take the chance.

Making up his mind, he rose and said, 'Excuse me for a minute. I will return shortly.'

A drunk patron was standing at the urinal, pissing mostly on his shoes, as Tan entered the men's toilet and went straight to the last cubicle. He glanced back at the drunk who was intent on improving his direction and knocked three times in rapid succession on the door. The drunk turned to watch, not improving his aim. The latch clicked and the door swung open slightly to reveal Diem, looking nervous but relieved to see his son. Tan nodded to his father and they made their way back out through the restroom door. The drunk watched them depart with some interest.

'So that's where they hide 'em?' he muttered to himself.

He managed to zip up his fly, stagger to the second last cubicle and mimicking Tan's signal, he gave three short knocks on the door.

'I know you're in there. Open the door.'

A gruff voice from within the cubicle growled, 'Fuck off, ya fairy!'

The drunk reacted haughtily, grunted and staggered out of the toilets.

Tan and Diem returned to the lounge where he introduced his father to Lyons, and they sat at the table. Tan explained to the others what had happened the previous night at Sam's restaurant and the subsequent car chase and their escape.

'They could have been anti-Vietnamese hooligans. Heaven knows, there are enough of them around,' Wey said.

'I do not think so, Mr Wey, it is too coincidental and ...' He paused and looked at his father, not having told him of the next bit of information. 'I had an *accident* at work today that could have been fatal. I was working under a truck and it suddenly fell on me.' Diem looked shocked as Tan added quickly, 'I was lucky. I was not hurt,' he quickly reassured his father. 'It could have been a faulty jack. But it could also have been engineered.'

Mr Wey looked disappointed. 'And you suspected that I was somehow involved? That is why you were reluctant to meet in my office tonight?'

'We had just come from seeing you, what was I to think?' Tan justified himself.

Wey was forced to concede this but tried to exonerate himself, 'Of course, but I can assure you ...'

Lyons interrupted him. 'I can personally vouch for Mr Wey. He has been of considerable help to us in the past. But I agree you are both at enormous risk.'

He turned to Diem.

'Mr Diem, it is essential that we get all the facts down on paper as soon as possible. Mr Wey has kindly offered to make his office available. If you and your son are agreeable?'

'You mean now, tonight?' Tan asked nervously.

Lyons nodded. 'My car's parked out the back. The sooner we get a statement the better. Then I can get straight onto it first thing in the morning.'

Tan and Diem looked at each other, silently asking for the other's approval. Diem nodded to his son and then turned to Lyons.

'Very well, Mr Lyons.'

'Good,' Lyons smiled, and the four men stood, preparing to leave.

Chapter 11

Several hours later Steve and Sally were still sitting outside watching the last of the customers leaving the hotel. Sally had nodded off to sleep in the passenger seat. Steve checked his watch again for the tenth time and suddenly unable to wait any longer said, 'Almost closing time,' as he opened the car door to get out.

The movement woke Sally with a start and she cried, 'Where are you going?'

'To check if he's still in there,' he said as he slammed the door shut and walked off towards the hotel.

'But Steve …' she called, but he was already out of earshot, halfway across the road and hurrying towards the hotel entrance.

He entered just as the staff were cleaning up and getting ready to close. He quickly looked around the almost empty bars and not seeing Tan, headed for the lounge. There was no sign of him there either or any other Asians so he had a few quick words with the barman who remembered Tan and Diem being there in the company of two other men but informed him they had left hours ago. Steve was angry and frustrated, wondering how they could have left without him or Sally seeing them. He hurried back to his car and told Sally that they'd disappeared and that Tan's utility was still parked where he'd left it.

'Well, maybe he's gone on somewhere with friends and they'll drive him back to his ute later,' she suggested.

'Sally,' Steve replied doubtfully as he got back into his car, 'from what I heard on the phone, he wasn't going out with friends.'

*

In Wey's office, the Chinese businessman entered, carrying a tray of coffee and sandwiches, laying them on the desk in front of Diem and Lyons, who was writing down the details of Diem's experience on board the *Luger* and his subsequent escape. Tan stood by the window, looking out into the street below.

'How is it going?' asked Wey.

Lyons hardly acknowledged Wey's intrusion, intent on his note-taking.

'Just about finished.' He looked up at Diem who was showing the strain of the interrogation. 'And what were the papers they provided you with?'

'Entry papers ... Migrant Visa.'

'In your name?' Lyons asked.

'No, in the name of Cao Van Lam.'

'Can I see them,' Lyons said, holding out his hand.

Diem looked at Tan saying, 'I do not have them with me ... My son thought ...'

'They are back at my flat,' Tan said. 'I did not think we should risk carrying them around ... Just in case.'

Lyons nodded in understanding. 'It doesn't matter,' he said. 'We can pick them up later. What's the address?' he asked preparing to write it down.

Tan gave him the street and flat number and Lyons jotted it down.

'I thought we could do with some refreshments,' Wey said as he passed around coffee and sandwiches. Lyons took his coffee and began to pace the room, thinking.

'When Mr Wey mentioned the ship involved was the *Luger*, I did some checking.' He moved back and faced Diem.

'She's in port. Here in Melbourne. She sails at first light tomorrow morning.'

Tan and his father shared an uneasy look.

'I want you to come down to the dock and identify the ship, the captain and the crew. All of them. Now. Tonight.' Lyons said.

Tan saw the immediate danger to his father and replied, 'No! You cannot expect ...'

But Lyons overrode him, concentrating his attention on Diem.

'I know it's a lot to ask but you are the only one who can positively identify them.'

'There must be another way!' Tan argued, 'Couldn't you ...'

'Not without running the risk of some of them getting away and alerting other members of the gang,' Lyons insisted. 'I've got a squad of Commonwealth Tactical Police on standby. We have the advantage of a surprise attack – if you give us the go-ahead,' he said looking straight at Diem for his agreement.

Diem looked at Tan and there was a long pause before he nodded and said, 'I must, for your mother's sake.'

Tan sighed and eventually relented but with a proviso, insisting, 'Then I must come too.'

Lyons nodded. 'Of course. You can look after your father during the round-up operation. ' He then turned to Diem reassuringly.

'Mr Diem, we'll look after you,' and then he smiled, 'we've got to. You're our only witness. And I want these bastards.'

He then picked up the phone and dialled.

'Well, it looks like it is all under control now and I will not be needed any further,' said Wey, as he shook hands with Tan and his father.

'Thank you for all your help, Mr Wey,' said Tan, 'and I am sorry I doubted you.'

Wey smiled and waved, dismissing the thanks.

On the phone Lyons was saying, 'This is Lyons, we have a go on that stake-out. Let's go for it.'

*

Meanwhile Steve was sitting in his living room, slumped on the settee, a mug of coffee on the table in front of him. He'd been sitting there for some time, lost in deep thought and obviously very worried about Tan's whereabouts.

103

Sally, dressed in a robe and ready for bed, entered and for a moment stood looking at him with concern. She walked to him and laid her hand on his shoulder. He jumped and looked up at her.

'Coming to bed?' she asked.

'In a minute,' he replied, picking up his coffee, 'Soon as I finish this.'

'Steve ...' she murmured, not quite knowing what she could say or do to ease his concern.

'I'll be there in a minute!' he responded impatiently.

Despondently, she turned and walked towards the bed room.

'I'm sure he's alright, Steve. He's not a child and he'd call you if he was in trouble.'

'If he can,' Steve replied. Looking at her worried face, he smiled gently and said, 'Sorry. You go in. I'll be there soon.'

*

Lyons pulled the car up at the port security gate. A storm was beginning to brew with the early rumbles of thunder and occasional flashes of lightning in the distance. He got out of the car and wandered over to have a word with the security guard on duty. Tan and Diem, sitting in the back passenger seats, watched him pull out his ID card and show it to the guard. After a brief discussion, the guard nodded and indicated where the *Luger* was moored. Lyons got back into the driver's seat and, dousing the headlights, drove slowly through the gates and into the dock area.

'It's all under control', he said quietly. 'The stake-out's on its way and should be here any minute.'

The car came to a stop in the deep shadow of a storage shed near the wharf. Silently, the three men got out of the car.

'Now keep as quiet as you can.' Lyons instructed them. 'Some of the crew might be hanging around.' He led them around the back of a shed and onto the wharf, keeping in the shadows. Suddenly Diem gasped as he saw the *Luger* for the first time since his escape. She was moored at the wharf, looking even more threatening in the darkness with the moonlight throwing shadows and an eerie light over the evil structure. In his mind it represented a ship of death. The ship looked deserted except for one of the crew who could clearly be seen on guard duty. He was smoking a cigarette and the puffs of smoke trailed up towards the rust encrusted and stained bridge, but he was not looking in their direction. He tossed the cigarette butt into the water and moved back away from the rail and out of sight.

Lyons quickly ushered them back into the dark doorway of the shed 'Quick, in here,' he whispered urgently.

As soon as they entered the shed Lyons closed the door and for a moment they were lost in the blackness.

Suddenly the shed blazed in light and the three men were confronted by the sneering grins of Brandwell, Ricketts and four other crewmen standing waiting for them. Tan was caught completely off guard and whirled around to face Lyons with a look of shock on his face. Lyons suddenly dropped the facade and became very business-like as he addressed the six sailors.

'Okay,' he said, 'let's get on with it.'

'You bastard!' shouted Tan, 'You mongrel bastard!'

'Well, I'll be buggered,' snarled Ricketts. 'If it ain't Steve Saunders' pet monkey.'

'Welcome back, Mr Diem,' smiled Brandwell evilly, 'It's time you and ya kid joined your old lady. Ya see we like to keep the family together.'

Brandwell, Ricketts and the four other sailors advanced on them menacingly. Tan stepped protectively in front of his father, determined to fight to the end. Behind him, Diem cringed in terror.

It wasn't much of a fight as Tan and his father struggled desperately but were hopelessly outnumbered and quickly overpowered by their six brutal and determined opponents.

Tan regained consciousness on board the fishing trawler, the *Shark*, as it made its way out into deep water. He had no idea where they were or how they'd got there. He vaguely remembered a car ride and being knocked out again when he had come to during the trip. His head and body ached from the beating he had received.

The speckled lights of a small settlement shone dimly in the distance through the mist. The night was dark with the occasional flash of lightning and clap of thunder as the storm abated to a light mist of rain that flurried across the deck on the wind. He was aware of being constrained and weighed down and realised he had been dumped on the deck under a pile of stinking fishing nets. He lay there for a few seconds trying to fathom his circumstances. He attempted to move his head with little effect with the heavy netting restraining much movement. Suddenly, in a flash of lightning, he realised he was staring into the face of his father. Diem was no longer unconscious – he was dead. His face was twisted and frozen in pain and it was apparent he had suffered a fatal stroke or heart attack. A crash of thunder extenuated Tan's horror and disbelief. Unable to accept that this could possibly have happened, Tan whispered, 'Cha?' but there was no reply. Grief and despair overwhelmed him and tears welled in his eyes as he realised the tragedy that had befallen his old father because of his own complicity, and he wept quietly.

Suddenly, from the bow end of the deck, Tan heard Hooker call out.

'Hey, Jimmy, give us a hand with these weights.'

'Okay,' Jimmy shouted back and it was obvious to Tan that he was quite close by.

He became aware of Jimmy's legs passing him, but quickly closed his eyes pretending to still be unconscious in case it was noticed but the sailor continued on without a glance and headed out of sight toward the bow. Tan started to struggle under the nets and realised he hadn't been bound! Obviously they'd believed the heavy netting and unconsciousness would be enough to hold him for as long as was needed. With great difficulty he struggled to disentangle himself until eventually he was free. He slowly rose to a crouched position, looking around to see if he was being observed but found himself completely alone on the stern end of the deck. He searched desperately for somewhere to conceal himself and saw on the other side of the deck another pile of nets, part of which was hanging untidily over the side of the trawler.

Suddenly from the bow end he heard the crash of metal weights and chain hitting the deck. Not daring to wait any longer, he darted across the deck and began to climb over the side next to the netting.

Hooker and Jimmy dragged the weights to the stern of the trawler where they'd left Diem and Tan.

'Right, let's have 'em,' said Hooker.

They began to pull the pile of nets away.

'Jesus, one of 'em's gone!' yelled Jimmy.

'He can't be! I checked 'em not more than five minutes ago!' Hooker yelled in disbelief.

'Well, he has!' Jimmy assured him. 'This one's not goin' anywhere though. He's carked it.'

'Shit!' screamed Hooker. 'Check the boat!' he yelled to the other two crewmen. 'The young one's shot through! Search the friggin' boat!'

The two other crewmen arrived on the run from the bow of the boat and frantically they all began to search but without success. Jimmy went to the rail near where Tan had climbed over and looked out to sea.

'He must've gone over the side.'

'This far out and in this weather?' Hooker replied disbelievingly. 'Don't be fuckin' stupid.'

'He knew he didn't have a chance anyway,' Jimmy argued. 'It'd be worth the risk.'

Hooker joined him and they stood peering into the blackness but saw nothing. Hooker turned away. 'Keep looking!' he ordered.

The search continued but it was soon obvious to them that Tan was not hidden on board so the captain and crew congregated on the forward deck very close to where Tan was hanging over the side, concealed under the netting and supporting himself on the gunwale that ran along the outside of the trawler's hull. The cold, black waves lapped his legs as he clung on desperately.

'Alright, the bastard must've gone overboard,' Hooker said to his crew. 'Now listen, he hasn't got a hope in hell of makin' it to shore in this weather and the freezin' water. So we're all gonna keep our mouths shut, ya hear me? As far as anyone's concerned, we threw 'im over the side with his old man, okay?'

The crew nodded and muttered their agreement.

'Right, let's make sure this one goes to the bottom – and stays there.'

They started to attach the weights to Diem's body with the chains and when they had finished they manhandled his body to the rail near where Tan was hiding and heaved it over. There was a huge splash and Tan was aware of his father's body crashing into the sea almost beside him and turned his face away, pledging an oath that he would avenge his mother and now his father's death.

The storm had passed and the sky was lightening with the approach of dawn as the *Shark* made its way into port. Weary with strain and shivering from the freezing cold, Tan still clung desperately to his hiding place under the netting hanging over the side of the trawler. He looked around and saw they were not far from shore and the growing light was putting him in danger of being seen. He decided to make a break for it before it was too late. He noticed another fishing boat at anchor nearby and as the *Shark* passed it, Tan slipped out of the net and swam underwater toward the other boat, surfacing out of sight of the *Shark*. He waited until the trawler was well past and then wearily but carefully, swam toward the shore.

Eventually he managed to reach the shore safely and weak and shivering lay on the beach for a few minutes recovering but the cold and determination drove him on. Keeping out of sight as much as possible he eventually found the highway and a truck stop service station and was able to hitch a lift with a truck driver who was heading for Melbourne and had stopped for breakfast in the dining room of the service station. The truck driver was suspicious at first of Tan's bedraggled appearance but, using all the charisma and charm he could muster, Tan explained that he was getting married the next day in Melbourne and his groomsmen and mates had played the usual trick on him and got him drunk at his buck's night and driven him fuckin' miles away and dumped him on the beach, as a buck's night gag. The driver, Ernie, a middle-aged family man who wasn't that strong in the brain department, thought it was a shockin' thing to do to a mate and gladly agreed to give Tan a lift along with some strong advice as to what he should do to his so-called mates when he caught up with them. It involved something to do with Senapod in their wedding breakfast meal. Tan agreed it was a good idea and managed to drop off to sleep for a couple of hours before he was delivered at Steve's garage.

Steve was appalled at Tan's condition and took him straight home to his house where he continued to berate him.

Upset and furious Steve paced around the living room in frustration. Tan was sitting, silent and contrite, on one of the lounge chairs, huddled in a blanket, and holding a hot cup of coffee.

'For God's sake, Tan, why didn't you talk to me about it? This is not the sea scouts you're mucking around with. This is organized crime! Murderers!'

'I am a grown man. I have my own responsibilities,' Tan argued. 'I am still Vietnamese and, as the only remaining son, it is my duty.'

'Jeesus,' Steve retaliated in frustration. 'We look out for each other! We're not just friends, goddammit, we're family too!'

Steve had become so emotionally upset, he turned away. Tan looked at him contritely but with great affection and for a while there was silence between them.

Then Tan sighed and said, 'In times of trouble my mother would say, "If I were a bird I would fly away to another day of my life." Now they have flown away together … to another life.'

Steve turned and looked at him and his anger dissolved. He walked over and laid his hand on Tan's shoulder.

'If I were in Vietnam,' Tan continued, 'I would go to the family altar and pray. Offerings would be made and their favourite dishes would be prepared …'

'We'll get the bastards, mate,' Steve said softly.

Sally entered from the kitchen with hot food and more coffee. She had left work immediately Steve phoned her that Tan was back.

'So, where do we go from here, the police or the Immigration Department?'

Steve sat on the settee and started pouring coffee for the three of them.

'And what do we tell them?'

'Everything. The whole story,' she said, thinking the question superfluous.

'Just think about it,' Steve said hopelessly. 'We haven't got a real shred of evidence. There are no bodies, no records of Tan's mother and father even having arrived here. It's only Tan's word. Who'll believe him?'

'They could search the *Luger*,' she said.

'And find what? Do you think these people don't cover their tracks?'

Tan suddenly remembered something. 'The papers. The false papers. The ones that were given to my father.'

Steve turned to him in surprise.

'You've still got them?'

'Hidden in the flat,' Tan replied, nodding in excitement.

A ray of hope shone for them all. Steve swigged down his coffee and stood.

'Sally, get some of my clothes for Tan.'

As they drove to Tan's flat, a silence fell over the three companions, each inextricably locked into the same predicament, each concerned about the other and the danger they were all in. Steve was still mulling over Ricketts' involvement.

Sally sat next to Steve in the passenger seat and Tan sat in the back passenger seat wearing some of Steve's clothes, a baseball cap pulled low over his eyes and a pair of dark sunglasses.

'Bloody Ricketts again, eh?' Steve fumed. 'Why doesn't it surprise me that he'd be mixed up in something like this?'

A thought suddenly occurred to Sally.

'Steve,' she said, 'what about the Navy patrol boat? Surely they would have reported the *Luger* was carrying illegal refugees?'

'I wonder,' he answered. 'There's a big question mark about that patrol boat too. Why would they just go off and leave the ship without keeping it under surveillance?'

'And why wasn't it impounded when it did reach port?' she added.

'Exactly,' he said. 'Ten to one it's a phoney.'

'But how could that be?' Tan interjected from the back seat.

'Navy surplus,' Steve said over his shoulder. 'If you've got enough dough, anyone can buy one, you know.'

'My God, it must be a huge organisation,' Sally said.

Steve nodded. 'With a lot of contacts in high places by the look of it. So we're going to have to be very careful who we talk to.'

When they reached the flat, Tan took his keys from his pocket to open the front door, but it wasn't necessary. The lock had been forced and the door swung open at his touch. The three exchanged concerned looks. Steve gently pushed the door and peered in, indicating Sally should wait outside while he checked it was safe to go in. He and Tan entered cautiously and looked around.

The place had been completely ransacked. Upturned furniture, torn books and clothing, smashed crockery and ornaments, littered the floor. Painting and photographs had been ripped from their frames and even the carpet had been ripped up in places. The intruders were long gone, and Sally followed Steve and Tan in.

'Jesus!' said Steve as they surveyed the destruction. 'They obviously knew what they were looking for.'

They looked at each other in dismay and then Tan rushed into his bedroom with the others following. The bedroom had received the same expert treatment. Tan rummaged through the clothing that had been pulled out of the wardrobe and strewn about on the floor and eventually found a particular shoe. He shoved his hand in but brought it out empty. He looked at Steve and shook his head in disappointment.

'Are you sure that's the right one?'

Tan nodded despondently.

'Right,' Steve suddenly flew into damage control. 'Get a few things together. One thing's for sure, you're not staying here. You're moving in with us.'

Steve moved to the window and looked out, checking to see if anyone might be watching the place but saw nothing obviously suspicious. Tan and Sally began to gather a few things together and pack them into a suitcase that hadn't been entirely ruined.

'What do we do now? Sally asked as she threw a couple of pairs of Tan's shoes into the case.

Steve shrugged and turned to Tan. 'Who else knew the papers were here?'

'That bastard who said he was from the Immigration Department, Lyons, and Mr Wey, maybe,' Tan said, pausing to think. 'But I don't think he was there during that part of the interview … I can't remember.'

'Mr Wey wouldn't be mixed up with people like this,' Sally said, defending her friend fiercely.

'Sally,' Steve almost had to spell it out for her, 'he introduced Tan and his father to this Lyons character.'

'Yes, I know,' she argued back, 'but Lyons *could* be working in Immigration. You said it yourself: *people in high places.*'

'Then Mr Wey could tell us where to find him. Whether he's involved or not, he's the logical place to start.'

Sally was worried about Steve becoming more personally involved.

'Steve,' she almost pleaded, 'let the police handle it.'

'And if he is involved, he'll deny knowing anything and we don't have a leg to stand on. And with what we know,' Steve added unnecessarily, 'we'll all be as good as dead.'

Either way the prospects looked bad to Sally.

Chapter 12

Later, in Chinatown, Steve walked along the street to the entrance of Mr. Wey's building. He stopped outside to check the floor and office numbers but he didn't notice Yin Foo, the Chinese street photographer, busily snapping shots of him from across the street. Steve entered the building and made his way to Wey's office, knocked and entered. Wey's Oriental female assistant greeted him. He introduced himself and asked if it was possible to talk with her employer. She politely excused herself, knocked on the door of Wey's office and entered. She returned a few moments later, smiled and ushered him into the office. Steve and Wey shook hands and the receptionist left the room.

'Thank you for seeing me,' Steve smiled as they sat at the desk.

'So you are the Steve that Sally has been telling me about,' said Wey, returning the smile.

'Not telling you too much, I hope.'

'Lovely young lady. She and I have had many dealings with each other.'

'Yes, that's why I'm here. She suggested I come and see you.'

'And what can I do for you?' Wey said, cocking his head slightly to one side.

'Well, I have this Vietnamese boy who works for me in my garage. He's been acting a bit strange for the last few days and now suddenly he seems to have just disappeared. He hasn't turned up for work and he's not answering his phone.'

'I see,' said Wey in a concerned tone. 'What is this boy's name?'

'Tan … Nguyen Tan.'

Steve watched closely for some reaction but Wey only appeared thoughtful and a little puzzled. Steve took a photograph of Tan from his pocket and handed it across the desk to Wey. After a few moments of scrutiny he placed the photograph on the desk in front of him.

'No, I don't know him,' Wey finally said, 'but I will ask around my friends in the Vietnamese community. Someone may have heard something.'

'Thank you, Mr Wey, if you would. I'm very worried about him,' Steve said, not giving any indication that Wey had just implicated himself.

'Did he talk to you about being in any sort of trouble?' Wey asked innocently.

'No, not at all. That's why I'm worried,' Steve replied, mirroring Wey's innocence.

Wey smiled a little patronisingly.

'Mr Saunders, I wouldn't concern myself too much if I were you. From my considerable experience I have found it to be an unfortunate fact that some of these Vietnamese boys can be very unreliable. They do tend to move to greener pastures without giving any notice.'

They spoke briefly for a few more minutes with both men trying unsuccessfully to sound the other out and Steve finally stood, ready to leave.

'Well, thank you for your time, Mr Wey. I thought I'd ask, but,' he shrugged, 'as you say …'

'Not at all,' Wey said, standing and shaking hands. 'I will ask around and let Sally know if I come up with anything.'

Steve smiled, thanked him and left the office. Wey watched him go, speculatively. He picked up the photograph of Tan, looked at it for a moment and slowly tore it in half and dropped the pieces into the waste paper basket by his desk.

*

At the house, Tan sat disconsolately in one of the chairs. Sally, smartly dressed for work, entered from the bedroom.

'Sorry I have to leave you but there are a couple of appointments I have to keep.'

'That's alright,' Tan said rising. 'I should go down to the garage.'

'You stay where you are,' she ordered. 'You're supposed to be dead. You heard what Steve said, you've got to keep out of sight.'

'For how long?' Tan groaned. 'I can't just sit around ...'

'Until we get enough evidence to go to the police.' she cut in.

'Sally, I don't want Steve to put himself in any – you know, danger – for my sake. I don't want to see him go back to the way he was.'

She secretly held the same fears.

'Well, we'll have to go on looking after him, without him knowing, won't we?'

'How can I do that when I'm stuck in here?' he complained.

'You have to be for the time being,' she said, 'but I don't.'

That didn't help Tan in the least but she didn't give him the chance to reply.

'By the way, those false papers they gave your father, what name were they in?'

He tried to remember. 'Cao Van Lam,' he replied. 'Why?'

Sally jotted the name down on a piece of paper and put it in her bag.

'Just curious. Get some rest. See you later.'

And with that she headed for the front door.

'Sally?' Tan called after her but it was too late. She'd already left, leaving a very frustrated and disgruntled Tan in her wake. He threw himself back on the chair with a groan.

*

Steve arrived back at the garage to find Splicer sitting dejectedly on the office step, waiting for him. 'You made of money?' he asked askance. 'You're late. Do you know how many customers I've had to turn away?'

'Sorry, something came up,' Steve replied as he set about unlocking the office, gas pumps and workshop while Splicer followed him like a pet cougar.

'I told 'em you had a recurring case of the clap that you'd caught in 'Nam. Thought it might make 'em feel sorry for ya so they'd come back.'

'Thanks,' Steve replied drily.

'It seemed to work,' Splicer said, 'except for the women.'

Steve ignored that and opened the workshop door. 'Su-Su's not finished yet,' he said regretfully.

'Doesn't matter,' Splicer replied disconsolately. 'I lost the job, anyway.'

Steve was genuinely contrite 'Sorry, mate, that's a real bastard, but I've had my own problems.'

'Them's the breaks,' Splicer shrugged, 'Where's Tan, anyway?'

'Had to go away for a few days,' Steve lied, but then had a sudden idea. 'Listen, seeing you're up on the blocks for a while, how would like to give us a hand here? You've done it before.'

Splicer perked up a bit. 'Fair dinkum? I mean, yeah, sure.'

'I might have to take a bit of time off m'self. If you could keep an eye on the place, you know, open and close up, look after the petrol and so on, it'd be a big help. You'll be paid of course.'

'Piece of piss,' Splicer agreed enthusiastically as they moved back towards the workshop.

*

Sally entered the Department of Immigration building and took the lift to the twenty-eighth floor. She entered the office marked 'Records' and looked around. Seeing the person she was looking for, she made her way over to the desk where Jennifer Burton, a friend of long standing, sat working at her computer. Sally stood behind her watching her work. Jennifer sensed her there, turned and smiled.

'Hi, Sally! What are you doing up this way?'

'Hi, Jen,' Sally replied, smiling her most winning smile. 'I need a bit of information – *off the record*,' she whispered.

Jennifer eyed her suspiciously.

'How much *off the record?* If you want to know if I've been getting any lately, that information is there for all the world to see.'

Sally laughed. 'I've already seen that written up in the ladies' room. No, I'm trying to trace a Vietnamese man by the name of Cao Van Lam. Apparently he's shot through from his last address and his wife is trying to find him. Maintenance, or something. Child support,' she added to make it more convincing. 'I thought you might have something on your records.'

'Bastards,' said Jennifer. She swung back to her computer screen and punched in a few keys. 'The trouble is, as you know, a lot of Vietnamese share the same family name so it's pretty common to find more than one with the same given name. Can be a bit confusing.' The screen opened on the file Jennifer was looking for. 'What was the name again?'

Sally showed her the piece of paper with the name written on it.

'Remember,' Jennifer warned, 'for God's sake, you didn't get this from me. This is classified for this office use only.'

Before Sally could respond, and unnoticed by the two women, Jennifer's boss, Gary West, entered on his way to his own office. He was an extremely good-looking man in his mid thirties, well groomed, tall, athletically built and dressed in very expensive, tailored clothes. His brown hair hung low over his tanned forehead and his eyes were a couple of shades darker than his hair. He stopped momentarily as he saw the two women staring at the computer screen.

'Ms Burton,' he called, and the two women turned guiltily to face him.

'My office please.'

'Right, Mr West,' Jennifer replied a little nervously. 'Won't be a minute.'

'Now, thank you,' he said curtly and waited for her to join him. She punched in a key to exit the programme and stood.

'Who's the hunk?' Sally whispered.

'My boss, Gary West,' Jennifer whispered back as she picked up a notepad.

'Cute,' said Sally.

'Forget it. I think he's a closet hermaphrodite.'

Sally smiled. 'Tried him?'

'We all have, from the tea lady to the office boy. Nobody's been able to get a rise, if you get my meaning. I'd better go. He's been in a shit of a mood for the last few days. I'll get that info to you as soon as the coast is clear.'

'Thanks, Jen, I owe you one.'

'Ms Burton!' West repeated, only more insistent this time, which caused Jennifer to scuttle away.

In his office, he asked who the girl was she'd been talking to and Jennifer replied that it was just a friend of hers from downstairs. 'From Ethnic Affairs', she quickly invented.

'What was she doing at your computer?' he asked.

'What?' Jennifer replied a little thrown, 'Oh, she wasn't *at* my computer, we were arranging a date ... tonight ... the movies.'

'The computer room is not for socialising, Ms Burton. You know the rules.'

'But she's on staff ... sort of.'

'Not *my* staff. See that it doesn't happen again, please.'

He leaned back into his chair, virtually dismissing her.

Jennifer was about to protest but thought better of it. She nodded obsequiously and returned to her desk.

*

Later that evening, Steve, dressed in dark overalls and carrying a tool bag, climbed a fire escape ladder at the side of the building next to Wey's office building and carefully eased himself onto the roof. After a few hair-raising moments of having to jump from one building to the next, which almost sent him crashing to the street below, he'd eventually made it to what he estimated was the area directly above Wey's office. He set about loosening a few slate tiles and then removed a torch from his bag and shone the beam into the darkness below. Satisfied, he removed a few more tiles and eased his way down through the hole he'd made.

Wey was sitting behind his desk working on some papers. He removed his reading glasses and rubbed his tired eyes. Standing, he moved to the window and looked out into the darkened street, now devoid of much traffic. In the ceiling above his desk, the manhole cover silently moved back to reveal a black slit. Through the slit, Steve's eyes surveyed the room.

The telephone suddenly rang and Wey cursed to himself and walked to the desk to answer it.

'Hello?' He waited while the caller quickly identified himself. 'Ah, all went well, I trust?' He listened for a moment and his face hardened.

'Yes, I did.'

It was obviously Lyons on the other end of the line and Wey immediately went on the defence.

'I tried to call you. I have them here … I sent a couple of men around last night …'

Lyons was obviously angry with him for exceeding his orders.

'How was I to know? I thought it was best to get them back as soon as possible.' His face flushed in anger as Lyons obviously abused him. 'I am not a child, Mr Lyons. I have just as much to lose as you.' Lyons obviously continued the abuse but Wey cut him off. 'Enough! You will have them back tomorrow. No, tomorrow!'

He slammed the receiver down in his anger. Through the manhole slit, Steve watched as Wey pensively removed an envelope from his desk drawer. Steve guessed it contained the false papers stolen from Tan's flat. For a moment Wey considered relenting and taking the papers directly to Lyons as he had requested on the phone. But then, annoyed at the way Lyons had spoken to him, he changed his mind and decided against it. He replaced the envelope in the drawer, locked it, took his jacket from a hanger next to the door and put it on, slipping his keys into the pocket. He then opened the door, turned off the lights and exited, locking the door behind him.

There was a silent minute's pause and then Steve slid the manhole back. A knotted rope tumbled from the hole and Steve began to climb down.

*

Tan was attempting to watch television as Sally entered from the kitchen, having just finished washing the dishes and cleaning up.

'Are you sure he didn't say how long he was going to be?'

Steve had left the house before Sally had returned home.

'No,' Tan said for the hundredth time. 'He just said to expect him home late.'

Sally checked her watch, also for the hundredth time.

'And he definitely didn't say where he was going?'

'No,' Tan replied impatiently.

At that point the front door opened and Steve entered, minus the overalls and tool bag. Relieved, Sally hurried to him and hugged him.

'Steve, where the hell have you been?'

In mock surprise he held her at arm's length.

'What? I got held up with Splicer. He's helping out at the garage until Tan comes back.'

'Till this hour?' she asked questioningly.

Steve smiled. 'So we had a few beers. Do I need a leave pass?'

'Did you get to see Mr Wey?' Tan asked from his chair, as he switched off the television.

'Yeah,' Steve replied, 'this afternoon. He's in it alright, up to his puffy Chinese neck.'

Sally was shocked and disappointed. 'No. Are you sure?'

Steve nodded and spoke directly to Tan.

'I showed him your picture and told him you'd been acting strange lately and then you'd just disappeared and we hadn't seen you since.'

'And?' Tan asked.

'Never seen or heard of you in his life. But he promised to check around for us. Says you Vietnamese are very unreliable types. Well, he was right there.'

'I can't believe it,' Sally responded, shocked. 'He's done so much to help the migrants. He was even honoured by the City Council last year.'

'Perfect cover,' Steve replied.

'You think he might have my father's false papers?' Tan asked.

Steve shrugged. 'I doubt it.'

'That reminds me,' Sally cut in, 'I did some sleuthing of my own today. I went to see a friend of mine at the Immigration Department.'

Steve and Tan both looked at her but before they could rebuke her for taking such a risk, she continued. 'Off the record,' she assured them. 'She's checking to see if there's a Cao Van Lam on their files.'

'What good will that do?' Steve said. 'It's probably a fictitious name anyway.'

'But is it?' Sally held up a cautionary finger. 'If this Cao Van Lam is a registered migrant, it could mean this Lyons character is getting the information from computer records and using actual names as a cover-up in case one of the illegals is ever picked up.'

'That's supposing Lyons is a bona fide investigator,' Steve reminded her.

'He is. I checked that too.'

'What? How?

'Easy,' she replied smugly. 'Immigration telephone extension numbers.'

Steve had to smile. 'What a clever, busy girl you've been.'

'And you thought I was just a gorgeous body,' she chided him.

'It seems that you two are doing all the leg work while I sit around watching TV,' Tan moaned.

'You get your chance tomorrow, my inscrutable little oriental man,' Steve smiled.

Tan and Sally looked at him questioningly.

'You're looking a bit pale and sickly lately,' Steve said to Tan in apparent concern. 'How would you like a nice boat trip?'

'Not if it's like the last one,' Tan replied.

Early the next morning, Steve and Tan launched the *Long Tall Sally* at the St Kilda marina. Sally joined them, bringing the gear they would need and soon they were navigating through the luxury yachts and pleasure boats and out into the bay.

'Now let's see if we can put all the chess pieces on the board,' Steve said. 'And the first one is the *Luger*.'

He throttled forward, the powerful outboard motor giving a satisfying roar as they shot forward and sped towards the Melbourne docks. The wind and spray, shooting out from the bow as it cut into the sea, added to his sense of purpose and resolve.

*

Wey's body smashed violently into the office wall. His face was bloody and swollen, evidence of the beating he had taken. Lyons stood over him, his face angry and twisted. Wey had sent his assistant out of the office on the pretext of buying some office supplies when Lyons had arrived. But when Wey told him he didn't have the false identity papers, Lyons had gone berserk.

'Let's have them, Wey,' he'd said threateningly.

'I told you, they were stolen!' Wey managed to scream through his busted lips.

'They weren't your property in the first place, asshole. Who *stole* them? Your mates from the Triad? Gonna use 'em to blackmail us, are they, shithead? This your way to get promoted, is it? No way, Wey.'

'Look at the drawer! You can see where it was broken into!'

Lyons spun around and studied the drawer and saw how it had obviously been forced. 'When did you see them last?' he barked.

Wey pulled himself up into a sitting position and tried to wipe the blood from his face with a handkerchief.

'Late last night, when you rang. I took them out of the drawer. I was going to bring them over to you like you asked, but I'd had a busy day ... I was tired and I had another appointment.'

Lyons dragged a chair over and sat staring straight into Wey's terrified eyes.

'They shouldn't have been in the fucking drawer in the first place. They should've been in the safe!'

'Nobody knew I had them ... I thought,' Wey said lamely.

'Obviously someone did. Has anyone been asking about the old man or the kid?'

Wey suddenly remembered Steve's visit and jumped at the chance to exonerate himself.

'His boss! The kid's boss! From the garage ... Saunders ... Steve Saunders!'

Lyons stared at him, then leant close.

'From the beginning – everything.'

*

The *Long Tall Sally* cruised into the port where the *Luger* was still docked. 'There she is,' cried Tan, pointing to the ship.

'Tan, out of sight, in the cabin, quick!' Steve said urgently. 'Let's take her in for a closer look.'

The cabin cruiser slowed down and moved in nearer to the dock.

'The wharves are very quiet,' said Sally.

Steve chuckled to himself. 'God bless the wharfies. They're obviously on strike again. That should keep her in port for a few days.'

He swung the boat out to sea. 'Well, we'll know where to lay our hands on her when we want her.' He glanced at Tan, crouching in the cabin. 'Now let's see if we can find that fishing trawler.'

*

At the garage, Splicer was serving a woman customer with petrol and checking the oil as Lyons drove up to the next pump and got out of his car. The woman paid Splicer and drove out. Splicer moved on to Lyons and said, 'G'day, fill 'er up?'

'Thanks,' Lyons said and casually walked away to check out the area while Splicer filled the tank. Satisfied, Lyons returned to Splicer.

'Are you Steve Saunders?'

'Nah. Steve's off for a couple of days. I'm just helpin' him out. D'ya want to talk to him?'

'Oh it's not urgent. I'll wait till he gets back. Couple of days, you said?'

'Yeah, he's taken his boat out fishin', lucky sod.'

Somehow suspicious, Lyons casually asked, 'Oh yeah? Which way is he heading?'

The automatic pump clicked off.

'Ah, didn't say.' Splicer looked at the gauge on the pump. 'Gees, ya didn't need much. Will I take it up to make it the even five dollars?'

Preoccupied and handing Splicer the money Lyons said, 'Thanks.'

'What's ya name? I'll tell 'im ya called.'

'It's alright,' Lyons said, 'I'll see him when he gets back.' And with that he got back in his car and drove off in a hurry, leaving Splicer looking puzzled.

*

They'd travelled several hours along the coast of south-western Victoria, past the fabled Twelve Apostles. It was a beautiful, clear day and the sea had been kind to them. Sally was at the helm while Steve studied a sea chart and Tan examined the shoreline through a pair of binoculars. Steve looked up from the chart and in the distance he could see a small fleet of fishing boats. He tapped Tan on the shoulder and pointed. Tan swung the binoculars around and studied the fleet but was unable to identify them from that distance. Sally set course for them.

Intent on the trawlers, Tan missed the bogus patrol boat anchored, camouflaged and shrouded in canvas, hidden in a small secluded inlet.

As they got closer to the trawlers, Tan squatted on deck, studying the fleet through the binoculars and soon ascertained the *Shark* wasn't amongst them. He shook his head, signalled his disappointment to Steve and Sally steered the boat back towards the shore.

*

At the Immigration Department, Gary West was standing at his filing cabinet when the door suddenly opened and Lyons stormed in. West turned abruptly to blast the unannounced intruder but suddenly recognised him. The colour drained from his face and he whispered harshly, 'Good God, what the hell are you doing here?' He rushed to the door and closed it firmly.

But Lyons was in no mood for niceties. 'Shove the security lecture. I think we've got trouble.'

*

126

The *Long Tall Sally* cruised into the very picturesque little harbour of Port Fairy. The sea was calm and reflected the images of several little pleasure boats at anchor. For a time they drifted around trying to see if the *Shark* was anywhere to be seen but without any luck. Steve was disappointed. 'Looks like we've drawn a blank here too.'

They pulled into a jetty and Steve and Sally disembarked and Tan passed up a couple of overnight bags.

'You book us in. I just want to tune the motor up a bit. Won't be long.'

Steve nodded and said, 'Try to keep yourself as inconspicuous as possible, will you? Mind you, with that head it won't be easy,' he laughed as he and Sally picked up the bags and headed for the entrance of the jetty.

They'd picked a motel close to the shore. It was fairly old and run down but they weren't looking for five-star accommodation just for one night. They certainly didn't get it. The motel was called 'The Whale Inn' and it was obviously a relic of the past. Although scrupulously clean, the decor was a little worn and featured much chintz and laminated surfaces. Mrs Lovett, the proprietor, matched the place admirably: a dumpy, middle-aged, formidably bleak woman who could well have been of the whaling period herself. Harpoons decorated the walls of the reception area together with other whaling paraphernalia.

'Rooms ten and eleven,' Lovett intoned like a Baptist minister delivering a eulogy as Sally and Steve booked in. 'Eleven's the double. Dinner is served in the dining room between six and eight, we are licensed, and neat, smart, casual dress is required.'

'Thank you,' Sally said, trying to hide a smile at the gargoyle's imperious manner.

'And the other gentleman will be arriving shortly?'

'Yes.'

'No pets, smoking, alcohol, cooking, eating or parties in the rooms, no television after eleven, and we hope you have a pleasant stay,' she added in her most insincere manner.

'Thank you, I'm sure we will.' Sally gave her the benefit of her most charming smile.

'Is there a disco or nightclub?' Steve asked innocently.

Mrs. Lovett paused, gave him a long, withering look, followed by, 'No, but we do have piped music in the dining room.'

'Oh, good!' Steve said in mock excitement.

'But no dancing,' she added, firmly.

'Right,' said Steve. 'I'm glad I didn't bring my dancing pumps.'

Sally gave him a nudge in the ribs with her elbow.

As they turned to escape to their room, they almost collided with two well-dressed Japanese men who were entering the reception area. They looked as out of place as Steve and Sally. Steve apologised and the two men bowed and stepped up to the counter.

'I do hope Dracula's mum doesn't double as the drink waiter,' Sally laughed as they made their way to their room. 'But just to be on the safe side, don't order anything red.'

'Her name may be Lovett, and she probably would, but she certainly ain't getting any of it by the look of her,' Steve said.

They opened the door into their room and stepped inside. It was clean but even more dilapidated than Sally had expected. 'So much for the romantic hideaway,' she groaned. But Steve hardly noticed as he dumped the bags and threw himself on the bed.

'What are you talking about? It's the cosiest place in town.'

He tried the bed springs and found them adequate as he bounced up and down. 'Do you think screwing is allowed in the rooms?' he leered seductively at Sally.

'Only if it's neat, smart and casual and before eleven pm,' she replied, echoing Mrs. Lovett's voice.

He pulled her to him on the bed and kissed her passionately but they were rudely interrupted by a loud banging on the door.

'My God,' Steve said as he jumped off the bed, 'she must have closed circuit TV in here.'

He went to the door and opened it expecting Mrs. Lovett with a shotgun but instead, Tan burst into the room, breathing heavily from running.

'The *Shark*!' he gasped. 'It's here!'

Steve turned to Sally in triumph.

The late afternoon sun was beginning to set over the hills as they arrived at a high vantage point overlooking the bay and looked down to see the *Shark* lying at anchor. A dinghy was pulling away from its side, heading for the jetty. On board were Hooker, with Jimmy, rowing.

Steve's attention was suddenly caught by the sight of the two Japanese men they'd seen at the motel reception who appeared to be walking onto the jetty to meet the incoming dinghy. One of the men was carrying a black leather briefcase.

Steve nudged Tan and indicated the men and they shared a puzzled look, wondering if there could be any connection. The dinghy glided to the jetty and one of the men stepped forward to help secure the mooring rope. Hooker disembarked and stepped ashore, smiling at the Japanese and shaking hands. They shared a few moments of what appeared to be friendly conversation and the trio began to walk back towards the motel. Steve, Tan and Sally were certainly puzzled by this new development.

*

Later, Steve stealthily made his way along the exterior of the motel until he came to the window of one of the units. He'd ascertained the unit number from reception, while Mrs Lovett was absent in the kitchen, no doubt slaughtering a bull for dinner.

The curtains were almost fully drawn except for a small slit between the two drapes where they hadn't quite connected. Taking care not to be seen, he put his eye to the gap and looked through. Inside the room, he saw Hooker and the two Japanese men sitting, drinking, smoking and chatting amiably, unaware they were being watched. Mrs Lovett will kill them if she catches them smoking and drinking, he thought. On the bed was the black briefcase. Hooker was speaking.

'Sorry about the hold-up gentlemen, but you know the Aussie wharfies. It looks like the dispute will be over tomorrow or the next day and the *Luger* can get underway. Should get you on board maybe tomorrow night, by the chopper.'

'We are not happy carrying this amount of money around for yet another day,' said one of the men referring to the briefcase. 'There is no safe in this ... establishment.'

Before Hooker could reply, the bedside phone rang and one of the Japanese answered it. After the caller had identified himself he replied, 'Ah, good afternoon Mr. West ... Yes, we have been told ... Yes he is, one moment please.' He handed the phone to Hooker. 'For you.'

'Yes?' Hooker said and listened as West warned him of the possible danger from Steve. 'Right,' he said, keeping his expression as neutral as possible, 'Okay, I'll keep an eye out ... No worries.'

He hung up the receiver and turned, smiling, to the two Japanese.

'Sorry, gentlemen, a bit of business just cropped up. I'll get back to you.' He downed the last of his beer and left the room. Outside, Steve moved away from the window.

When he returned to their room, Steve found Sally talking on the phone. She turned and smiled at him and he grabbed a pair of jocks from his bag and, indicating to her that he was going to take a shower, disappeared into the bathroom and began to undress. Sally returned her attention the phone.

'I see,' she said to the caller, 'Yes, that's a great help, Jen ... No, not a word. As I told you, it really only has something to do with a domestic situation I'm working on … Thanks again … Be in touch.'

She hung up the receiver and wandered into the bathroom, where Steve was under the shower and washing himself briskly.

'Where's Tan?' she asked.

'Keeping an eye on the trawler. Looks like it's pulled in for the night. Who was that on the phone?'

'Jennifer Burton,' she replied. 'That friend of mine from Immigration, she got the information we were after.'

'Oh, yeah?' Steve said over the noise of the shower.

'There are actually three Cao Van Lams listed on the records: one in Townsville, one in Taree and one in Warrnambool. All deceased.'

Steve thought about it for a moment then stuck his head through the shower curtain.

'They're using doubles – counterfeit papers in the name of registered migrants. Make it twice as hard to check up on them if one was picked up and questioned.'

'And you realise what that means?'

'Someone has access to the records,' Steve replied, and retreated back under the shower.

'Our friend Lyons?'

'Maybe,' he yelled from under the water, 'or someone higher.' He stuck his head out again. 'Will you get my shaving gear out of my bag? It's in the side pocket.'

She wandered over to his bag and fossicked through it. Eventually, she found his wet-pack and pulled it out, unintentionally dragging an envelope out at the same time. She dropped the envelope on the bed and took the wet-pack into the bathroom and placed it on the shelf.

'It's on the shelf,' she called and returned to the bedroom.

'Thanks,' he replied, 'be out in a minute.'

She sat on the bed to unpack Steve's bag and noticed the envelope. She picked it up, her face draining of expression, as she read the name on the front of the envelope 'Cao Van Lam'.

Slowly she removed the papers from the envelope and started to read, her expression hardening.

Chapter 13

From his vantage point, concealed from view from the *Shark*, Tan watched as Jimmy and the remaining two crew members piled into the dinghy and pulled for shore. What he didn't realise was that from a different vantage point, someone was watching *him* through a pair of binoculars.

Hooker slowly lowered the glasses and stood, planning his next move. 'Gotcha!' he muttered to himself.

Freshly showered and shaved, Steve returned to the bedroom, grabbed a pair of jeans from the bed and started to put them on.

'So it looks like these two Japs must be bagmen for the organisation. They're carrying a stack of dough in that briefcase …'

His voice trailed off as he noticed Sally sitting on the bed with the false papers in her hand. For the moment she couldn't even look at him. There was a long, strained pause before she spoke.

'How long have you had them?'

Guilty of misleading her, he headed for his bag and took out a dark T-shirt, with long sleeves.

'Since last night … I broke into Wey's office,' he finished lamely.

She looked at him coolly. 'You never intended going to the police, did you?'

'Yes,' he answered defiantly, 'eventually.'

'When?' she almost shouted at him, 'After you'd rounded them up single-handed? Or were you going to wipe them all out? Is that what we're really here for? Revenge? A vendetta?'

'No! Yes! …' He shook his head, his voice softening.

'In a way. But not just for Tan and his family's sake ... for *all* of them!'

Sally stared at him, not understanding. With emotional difficulty, he tried to explain. He dropped the shirt and turned to her.

'Have you ever seen a *real* refugee? Not the ones who were lucky enough to escape from the nightmare. I mean the ones who are *living* it.' He looked at her. 'The ones who have just had their homes and villages bombed – napalmed: for years watching their families, their kids and their friends, killed, tortured – butchered. I have. I saw them the first day I arrived in 'Nam, a couple of hours after I stepped off the plane.' He took a deep breath, as the memories flooded back.

'There was an old woman, she looked about eighty ... she was probably about sixty ... She had this little kid, I think it was a little girl, I couldn't tell ... The kid's face was mutilated ... A bleeding stump where she used to have an arm ... A filthy rag wrapped around it to stop the bleeding. The little kid had just seen her mother raped and her guts ripped out with a bayonet ...'

Sally shuddered.

'But their eyes,' he continued, amazed at the remembered horror, 'There was always this frightening ... acceptance ... The way life is ... Not fury, injustice or even sadness, just acceptance.'

Sally sat transfixed by the quiet, open, rawness of his emotion. Steve forced himself back from the path that had led him to hell. He looked at her.

'I saw that. I was a part of that. And now, some of them escape ... to what? Another nightmare? Slavery? Another unmarked grave? Another *acceptance* ?' He shook his head. 'I've got to undo at least some of what I was a part of.'

Awkward and unable or unwilling to continue, he picked up his jacket and headed for the door.

'I've gotta go and relieve Tan.'

Before Sally could speak, he was gone. Momentarily stunned she could only sit there thinking about what he'd said and the danger he was putting himself in. Eventually she rose and followed him out. She caught up with him outside the motel and called out for him to wait. Reluctantly, he slowed down and waited for her.

She drew level with him and placed her hand on his chest, her voice almost pleading with him.

'Steve, I do understand how you feel about those people and I can't imagine what it did to you having to experience it, but you've got to let the authorities handle it.'

'The *authorities*?' he scoffed loudly, which made her turn and check to see they weren't being overheard. 'Who, the politicians? The ones who make the decisions to send countries to war? The generals whose lives are shaped by war? The police, the power players, with the corruption that eats away at the system? They don't care about the people. Did you know when the Brits *liberated* Vietnam, or French Indo-China as it was then at the end of the Second World War, they re-armed the Japanese to fight the People's Liberation Front until the French could move back in and take control? They re-armed the men who had raped, slaughtered, maimed and tortured the population for years to fight the people who just wanted to run their own country? That's how it all started. Then the Americans needed a friendly base for their forces in South East Asia and they backed the wrong side …'

'But that's all over now. The war is over!' Sally argued.

'Not mine!' he replied fiercely as he turned and strode off toward the village.

She again followed him, waiting and praying he'd calm down. Eventually they came to a park and he sat on a bench. She stopped and looked at him for a sign that his storm had abated. He returned her look, sighed and smiled. She sat by him on the bench and took his hand.

'Look,' he said, 'I'm not trying to do this single-handedly. We've got the phoney papers, we know where the *Luger* is and now we know where the *Shark* is. The *Luger* isn't going anywhere while the strike is on so if Tan and I can cripple the

Shark we can make sure she stays here long enough for us to phone or get back to the city and hand the lot over to the proper authorities.'

'And that'll be it?' she asked.

'Yes,' he assured her earnestly.

Sally was still uneasy but before she could voice her concerns, Steve looked past her and his eyes hardened. She turned to see the sudden cause of the change in his expression. Coming out of the police station across the road, she saw the local cop and Hooker, chatting amiably. Steve turned her face to his, 'You still want to hand it over to the cops?'

She paused looking into his eyes, her mind whirling in trepidation. Finally and against all her instincts, she relented.

'Okay, we'll do it your way.'

He smiled at her gratefully and they watched as Hooker and the cop strolled off down the street together, laughing and chatting.

Sally, Steve and Tan left the dining room after dinner and nodded at Mrs Lovett in passing as they headed for their rooms.

'Oh, Mrs Lovett,' Sally said, stopping, 'we'll be leaving early in the morning so I'd like to fix up our account now, if that's okay with you?'

'Certainly,' the prim proprietor replied. 'If you'll just follow me through to Reception?'

She waddled off and Sally followed, telling Steve and Tan she'd see them back in the room. 'The dinner was … memorable, Mrs Lovett,' Sally said, for want of a better word, 'so … home cooked. The whole place is just … charming. Steve and I have just adored it,' she continued, on a roll of mock enthusiasm she couldn't seem to stop. 'Now we know you're here, we plan to come back often. It's so … refreshing.'

Mrs Lovett almost allowed herself to smile as they reached the counter and Sally handed over her credit card.

'Well,' she replied, 'being the oldest establishment in town, we try to make it unique.'

'And you certainly have,' Sally agreed somewhat drily and then added casually, 'I noticed a few fishing trawlers at anchor in the bay. We saw one come in this afternoon, the *Shark*, I think it was called. Do the crews stay here in town or do they just camp on the beach?'

Lovett gave her a supercilious smile. 'No, they mostly rent some of the old whalers' cottages. Nice gentlemen, of course, but not quite up to the standard of our clientele.' She handed Sally the docket to sign.

'Obviously,' Sally concurred. 'A little rough for those lovely chintz curtains and bedspreads. Well,' she said, before Mrs Lovett could respond, 'off to bed. Probably won't see you before we leave in the morning. I can't wait to climb in between those wonderful, pink and white floral sheets … Goodnight.'

'Oh, and you won't forget to turn down the spread, will you?' Mrs Lovett added as Sally walked away.

Sally stopped, turned back and smiled. 'Would I dare?'

Sally and Steve found it hard to sleep as they lay in bed thinking about the coming plan they would put into practice just before dawn.

Sally lay on her side facing Steve who was on his back with his head resting on his folded arms.

'I volunteered to go to 'Nam for the paper, you know?' Steve suddenly said.

'No, I didn't,' Sally said.

He nodded. 'I hadn't been called up and I was too old for conscription but I wanted to experience a war like my dad had. But I wasn't prepared to kill. The last of the "good" wars, he used to call it. The Japs were invading and he knew what he was fighting for, defending his home and his family and his way of life. He was proud of what he did.'

'And you weren't proud of him much?' she said smiling at him.

Steve smiled back.

'He couldn't kill a chook for Xmas dinner, but single handed he wiped out a whole Jap machine-gun nest. He used to say that going to war to defend his country was probably the most important thing in his life.'

'That must've made your mother happy,' she said wryly.

'Oh, he was crazy about her.' He smiled at the memory.' 'He told me once, whenever he looked at her, his guts smiled.'

Sally laughed gently. 'Now I know where you get your romantic streak from.'

Steve smiled back at her but he knew exactly what his father meant.

He glanced at his watch. 'Be dawn soon.'

She tried not to show the concern she felt.

'Time for us to go and start winning your war, huh?' She laid her hand on his chest and looked apprehensive. 'Steve …'

'Don't worry,' he put his finger to her lips. 'Tan and I are mechanics: piece of piss.'

In the early light, just before dawn, Steve and Sally joined Tan at the jetty. The town seemed deserted and the chilly morning mist lent a stillness to the surroundings. The water was calm and silent. They all wore warm jackets and Tan had the hood of his coat turned up over his head.

'Anyone go aboard last night?' Steve asked him.

'Not that I saw,' replied Tan. 'It was pitch black but I didn't see any lights.'

Steve nodded. 'We'll take their dinghy,' he said indicating the craft gently bobbing at the end of the jetty. 'It's a good indication they all stayed ashore last night and it will keep them ashore until we're finished. And it will save the noise of starting up the *Long Tall Sally*.'

Tan nodded, stowed their bags, got a tool-bag from their boat and they headed towards the dinghy. Sally, following Steve's instructions, boarded the *Long Tall Sally* to watch and wait.

'Keep an eye on the shore in case someone comes along,' Steve whispered before he left. 'We'll only be a few minutes and then we'll be on our way back to the city and report the whole thing, okay?'

She nodded uncertainly.

They boarded the dinghy and silently rowed out to the *Shark*, silhouetted in the near distance. As they drew near, Steve suddenly saw a small, dark shape lying in the water at the stern of the trawler. As they got close enough to pull alongside, the dark shape drifted around the hull into their view, just as their dinghy bumped gently against the side of the *Shark's* hull.

'It's another dinghy! Steve hissed at Tan. 'They've got another dinghy! There must be somebody on board.'

In answer to his calamitous discovery, their little boat was suddenly illuminated in a blinding light, similar in strength to a searchlight, it seemed. The *Shark's* motor roared into life and a figure appeared from behind the ships rail holding a bottle of gasoline with a lit cotton wick: a Molotov cocktail!

Steve and Tan had both stood up, preparing to board, and the sudden shock caused Tan to stumble against Steve. Steve, in his surprise, lost his balance and fell overboard just as the man on deck raised his arm and threw the burning Molotov cocktail straight into their dinghy. There was a dull explosion and the flames rode on the back of the spewing petrol, engulfing Tan who had fallen into the well of the dinghy, which became a flaming inferno. He jumped to his feet, screaming.

Steve surfaced just in time to see Tan rising to his feet, screaming and burning. For a second he stared in horror as the scene seemed to unfold in slow motion. In his mind it became intercut with the subliminal flashes of the burning boy of his nightmares. His face contorted in terror and he screamed, 'Nooooooo!'

Tan's burning body slowly seemed to topple and fall into the water, extinguishing the flames immediately. The stern of the trawler began to swing around, bringing the propeller closer and closer to Tan. Shocked into action, Steve floundered his way to Tan and tried desperately to drag him clear of the whirling propeller.

On board the *Long Tall Sally*, a panic-stricken Sally started the engine, slammed the throttle forward and roared towards Steve and Tan. Tan was unconscious as Steve supported him in the water, just managing to avoid the trawler's spinning prop which swept past with only inches to spare. The trawler attempted a sluggish turn intent on coming around to make another attempt to ram Steve and the unconscious young man he was supporting. The *Long Tall Sally* arrived alongside the two men in the water and Sally threw the engine into neutral and rushed to help them. With difficulty she managed to help Steve drag Tan aboard with Steve quickly following. As he hauled himself aboard, he looked up and saw the trawler coming out of the mist and bearing down on them. He screamed a warning to Sally who immediately saw the danger and flew to the controls, opened the throttle, and the *Long Tall Sally* shot forward out of the trawler's path. The *Shark* again attempted a turn to come around and ram them and Steve screamed, 'Get the hell out of here!' Needing no further urging, Sally opened the throttle fully and headed for the port entrance and the open sea. A much slower vessel, the *Shark* fell slowly behind.

The sun was now beginning to rise as the *Long Tall Sally* sped along the coast. In the cabin, Steve had grabbed the first-aid kit and was attempting to slather burn cream on his unconscious friend. He huddled, cradling Tan's body in his arms, willing him to live.

'Don't die! Please don't die … Not this time …'

'Steve!' Sally called over the roar of the engine. There was no response so she called again, louder and even more urgently. He looked up.

'Where to?' she cried.

Steve desperately tried to pull himself together. He shook his head trying to clear his thinking.

'Ah … hospital … The nearest town where they have a hospital!'

He gently laid Tan down on the bunk and grabbed a chart, working out their position and the nearest likely town.

'Here,' he said, taking her the chart and pointing. 'It's inland a bit but we'll get them to send an ambulance.'

He scrambled for the radio and switched it to transmit.

'Mayday, mayday … This is the *Long Tall Sally*! Somebody come in … mayday, mayday!'

There was a short pause and then a voice came over the speaker. 'Receiving you, *Long Tall Sally* ....This is the RAN Coastal Patrol. What is your position? Over.'

Steve sighed in relief and gave the co-ordinates. 'We have a badly burnt man on board. We need your assistance,' he yelled over the roar of the engine. 'Can you contact the nearest hospital and get them to send an ambulance to …' he checked the chart, giving them the co-ordinates. 'We'll meet them there – Over.'

'Wilco, *Long Tall Sally* … Stand by,' came the reply.

Sally smiled nervously at Steve.

'You alright?' she asked, desperately trying to tell how he was handling their situation.

He nodded.

'How's Tan?'

'Still unconscious. But he's breathing. Pulse is a bit erratic …Shock … Badly burnt.'

'Hello, *Long Tall Sally*, *Long Tall Sally*, come in, over,' the radio crackled.

Steve grabbed the microphone.

'*Long Tall Sally*, Saunders here, over.'

'No hospital for miles, Mr Saunders. We have you in sight. Heave to and we'll take the patient on board. We have a medical orderly on board who can take care of him until we get him to hospital. Over.'

Steve and Sally turned and in the distance, closing fast, they saw a Navy patrol boat approaching at high speed. Sally heaved a sigh of relief.

'Thank God.'

Steve took the wheel over from her, cut the motor back to idle and the cabin cruiser slowed to a stop, rocking in the water.

From on board the patrol boat, the *Long Tall Sally* lay straight ahead, drifting in the open sea. Beside the helmsman, Captain Bryce stood, staring straight ahead, eyes fixed on his prey.

'Hate breaking radio silence,' he said to the mate, 'but this won't take long.'

Steve and Sally watched as the patrol boat came closer and closer. Steve began to frown, a niggling suspicion beginning to form in his mind.

'She's coming in fast,' he said, becoming concerned.

The patrol boat roared straight at them as, almost too late, the realisation hit Steve.

'Jesus, it's the fake one!' he screamed. 'Hang on!'

He slammed the throttle forward and at the last second, swung the wheel, just managing to save them from being rammed. The patrol boat flashed past and was forced to make a wide turn to bring it around for a second attempt.

'What are we going to do?' Sally screamed.

'Give it as small a target as possible,' he called back. 'Get a life jacket on and try to get one on Tan!'

He grabbed the microphone again and yelled into it, 'Mayday! Mayday! Mayday!

On board the patrol boat, the helmsman once again lined up on the cabin cruiser and opened the throttle. Bryce stared coldly ahead and then turned and nodded to the mate and a couple of his crew who were standing nearby armed with automatic weapons.

Steve replaced the radio microphone and prepared for the next assault by heading the bow directly towards the oncoming patrol boat and holding his hand on the throttle, planning to swing away again at the last moment. This time there was a blast of gunfire from the patrol boat, whipping up the water in a trail of fire like deadly pebbles skipping across a pond towards the *Long Tall Sally*. But because of the speed they were travelling and the relatively small target, the gunfire went wide and just as it looked as though they would ram, Steve throttled hard, swerved out of the way avoiding a collision by inches and headed towards the shore and shallow water.

He searched the coastline looking for some sort of cover but they were near the Twelve Apostles and the water around was treacherous. Sally watched the patrol boat as it swept out to sea to make another turn. Suddenly, to her astonishment, she saw it make an abrupt change of course and head back up the coast away from them, in a westerly direction.

Hardly believing her eyes, she yelled excitedly, 'Steve, they're going! They're giving up!'

Surprised, he turned and said, 'What the hell?'

Once again he turned east and suddenly saw the reason for the patrol boat's hasty retreat. Heading toward them was another ship. He turned to Sally and said, laconically, 'I hope they couldn't afford a bloody frigate!'

As the ship came closer, Steve recognized a large number 45 painted on the grey bow of the ship. 'My God,' he said, 'it's the *Yarra*! – The *HMAS Yarra*! I saw her in 'Nam!' Then he suddenly remembered, 'I think she carries a helicopter on board.'

The *Yarra* hove to and dispatched a rigid-hull inflatable to the *Long Tall Sally*. Lieutenant Cooper came aboard with a doctor from the frigate. While the doctor attended to Tan, Steve tried to explain to Cooper what had happened.

'We knew there were no coastal patrol ships in the area,' Cooper said, 'and, when we heard your Mayday call and the exchange of signals, we realised something was very wrong. So we maintained radio silence and came to investigate.'

'Thank God you did,' replied Steve, 'it was getting a bit hairy.'

'It's lucky for you, Mr Saunders, we were in the area. We've been on exercises in Bass Straight and developed a minor problem and were ordered back to Williamstown for repairs. Before we arrived we intercepted the radio signals.'

Sally was very relieved to know that at last they were getting help from someone in genuine authority.

'What happens now, Lieutenant?' she asked Cooper.

'Well, Miss Grimes, we'll attend to your friend and then get after that patrol boat.'

'But you will report what's happened to the proper authorities?'

'Of course, as soon as I get back on deck,' he replied.

Sally looked at Steve and smiled in relief. He nodded in unenthusiastic submission.

The doctor joined them and reported to Lieutenant Cooper, 'He's holding on, but I'd like to get him to the Alfred hospital in Melbourne a.s.a.p. They're experts on burn cases. I think the chopper will do the trick.'

'Good,' said Cooper. 'We'll get that organised and then get after that patrol boat.'

They gently transferred Tan on board the *Yarra* and Sally and Steve watched as the helicopter took off heading for Melbourne and the *Yarra* set off after the phoney patrol boat. Only then could they relax and take stock of the situation.

'Well, you've finally got what you were after,' Steve said.

Sally put her arms around him. 'You've been absolutely marvellous. I'm so proud of you.'

'You didn't do too bad yourself,' he smiled.

'How are you feeling now?' she asked, looking at him closely.

He paused, trying to assimilate his thoughts and feelings.

'Now that it's over, not bad ... I guess the adrenalin's still pumping.'

'You'll probably have a slump soon, you know?'

Steve nodded. 'So, we'd better get back before that happens, eh?'

'I'll drive, you lie down and relax,' she said going to the controls. 'Remember, nice slow, deep breaths.'

She started the motor and eased the throttle forward.

'Keep well clear of those,' he said pointing to the Twelve Apostles as he reclined on the bunk. 'If we pile up on one of those, you'll have to save yourself ... and me.'

'You know, 'she said, moving into a lecturer mode to distract him, 'they were originally called the Sow and Piglets; the Sow was Mutton Bird Island, and the Piglets were the smaller surrounding islands. They were formed by erosion of limestone of the original coast line. The constant action of the sea on the limestone slowly, over thousands of years, wore down the original rocky cliff and left the individual pillars. You know, the cliff is still being eroded at the rate of two centimetres a year, so it'll just go on forming new apostles.'

She glanced over at Steve but he was already asleep.

Chapter 14

Sally sat in one of the chairs of the waiting room at the Alfred Hospital, watching Steve as he paced the floor. Any movement in the corridor caught his attention and he went to check. She rose and went to him trying to put her arms around him to comfort him but he pulled away.

'I really ballsed it up again, didn't I?'

'No, you didn't,' she tried to reassure him. 'It was a risk we all decided to take and it went wrong, that's all.'

'No, you were right. I should've handed it over ...'

He was interrupted by a nurse accompanied by a Chinese gentleman in his early forties, wearing a suit and tie that had seen better days. He was rather tall for a Chinese and slim, with a craggy face which conveyed authority. He was not a man to mess around with.

'How is he?' Steve asked the nurse, disregarding the Chinaman.

'No word yet, I'm afraid,' she replied. 'They're still working on him.'

Steve turned away in frustration.

'Mr Saunders, this gentleman would like to talk to you.'

Steve turned back, noticing the man for the first time.

'Mr Saunders, my name is Yin Foo,' he said, taking his ID from his pocket and showing it to Steve. 'Detective Sergeant Yin Foo – Commonwealth Police.'

Steve and Sally shared a look. Could a man with the name like Yin Foo, claiming to be a Commonwealth Detective Sergeant be for real, or was this yet another phoney?

*

Gary West, dressed only in a bathrobe, opened the front door of his apartment to a very agitated Glen Lyons, who pushed past him and stormed into the living room.

'Hooker lied to us!' he shouted in fury. 'Those two bloody Viets he was supposed to get rid of – the kid got away!'

West hastily closed the door and followed him. 'For God's sake, keep your voice down!'

'He turned up at the rendezvous this morning, at first light – with his boss, Steve Saunders!' He jabbed an accusing finger at West. 'I warned you.'

'What happened?' West asked him.

'They tried to get on board the *Shark*. Hooker and his crew were waiting for them. And they botched it up again! They think they got the kid this time but Saunders got away in his boat!'

West turned away in disgust. 'Why didn't Hooker call in the patrol boat?'

'He did!' Lyons retaliated fiercely. 'But Saunders managed to get past that! The last message Hooker got from Bryce was that the bloody Navy was on their tail!'

'Shit!' said West. 'Where are Hooker and the *Shark* now?'

'God knows – hiding out somewhere. Does it matter? The shit's hit the fan, Gary. It's time to get out.'

West thought desperately for a few moments but eventually nodded philosophically. Lyons headed for the door.

'I'll organise the chopper. An hour?'

'Make it two,' replied West. 'I've got some loose ends to tie up.'

Lyons nodded and left. West headed for his bedroom.

*

It was eventually revealed that Detective Sergeant Yin Foo was the man in the street in Chinatown pretending to be a street photographer. The hospital had arranged an office/consulting room for them to talk. Sally sat in one of the chairs while Yin Foo sat at a desk with Steve sitting opposite speaking on the telephone. Steve listened while the person on the other end of the line confirmed Yin Foo's identity.

'Thank you, I appreciate your help.' He hung up the receiver and looked across at Yin Foo.

'Satisfied?' Yin Foo asked.

Steve nodded. 'Sorry, but I had to check. This mob seems to have contacts everywhere.'

'I understand,' Yin Foo said. 'Naval Intelligence contacted us this morning. Now,' he said leaning across the desk and making notes in a yellow pad, 'what have you got?'

Steve paused as he looked across the room at Sally.

'A lot, but before we tell you, I've got one stipulation.'

'And that is?' asked Yin Foo, not amenable to any stipulations.

'I want to be in on it through to the end.'

Yin Foo sighed. 'Mr. Saunders, I understand how you feel but ...'

'Or,' said Steve, over-riding him, 'I only give you enough to go one step at a time ... with me in tow.'

'Steve ...' Sally tried to dissuade him, but he interrupted her.

'They owe me.' Steve looked levelly at the Chinaman. 'That's the deal.'

Yin Foo looked displeased at being pressured by an amateur but couldn't ignore Steve's determination.

'There isn't much time,' Steve urged him.

As much as he didn't like it, Yin Foo was forced to consider.

*

Gary West came out of his bedroom wearing a suit and vest and carrying a camel hair overcoat, felt hat, suitcase and leather briefcase. He put his luggage down by the front door, looked around his apartment, crossed to the telephone and dialled. After a few rings the call was answered. Without preamble, he said, 'I'm leaving now. I'll see you there in twenty minutes.' He hung up the phone and stood for a moment, looking around.

Suddenly he exploded into action and appeared to go berserk. He upturned furniture, tore paintings off the wall and smashed lamps, generally demolishing the place, making it look as though it had been ransacked. Finished to his satisfaction, he stood, breathing heavily, and surveyed the carnage. He then took a pen-knife from his pocket, opened the blade and deliberately ran it across his forearm. The blood began to ooze from the wound and he smeared it over a piece of broken mirror and flicked a few drops around before taking a plaster from his pocket and covering the small flesh wound. He then calmly walked to the door, put on his coat, pulled his hat down low over his eyes, picked up his cases and exited the room leaving the door slightly ajar behind him. When the police investigated his disappearance they would assume he had been robbed and abducted and possibly killed.

*

Yin Foo sat at the desk with the counterfeit papers on the desk in front of him. In his hand was the morning edition of *The Age* newspaper. The headlines read, 'Chinese Community Leader Dies in Chinatown Blaze.' He handed it to Steve and Sally rose to read it over his shoulder.

'Of course,' Yin Foo said, 'if you had come to us in the first place, your friend might not be lying in there fighting for his life, his father might still be alive and that,' he said, referring to the headlines, 'might have been avoided.'

Steve looked up from the newspaper.

'We had no hard evidence.'

'We didn't know about those papers until Steve … found them,' Sally added.

'And Tan didn't tell us about his father until after he was dead,' Steve reminded him. 'We were going to tell you this morning,' he added lamely.

'After you single-handily rounded up the entire operation?' Yin Foo remarked sarcastically.

'No!' Steve replied vehemently. 'Besides, we didn't know who we could trust.'

'We've had our eye on Mr Wey for some time,' Yin Foo said, looking at the phoney papers. 'His visible business activities didn't match up with his apparent income. We suspected he was tied up with a Triad. We also needed hard evidence.'

'I just can't believe Mr Wey was involved,' Sally said, looking askance at the headlines. 'He was always so – helpful and – kind.'

The phone rang and Yin Foo answered, 'Yes? … I see … When?' He looked at Steve as he talked. 'Is there any way of forcing them back?' His expression showed frustration as he listened to the caller at the end of the line. 'I see. Thank you.' He replaced the receiver and looked at Steve and Sally. 'The *Luger* left port early this morning. By now she'll be out into international waters. It would seem we've lost her.'

Steve was thunderstruck, 'But she can't be! What about the dock strike?'

'It was suddenly called off, first thing this morning,' Yin Foo replied cynically. 'It seems you are right, Mr Saunders, influence in very high places, and at very high prices, I would say.'

*

A helicopter stood on the heliport on the Yarra River warming up its engine. Gary West arrived in a taxi and hurried to the chopper pilot who was standing near the machine. Over the roar of the blades the pilot shouted, 'Where's the other bloke? I was told to expect two of you.'

'He'll be here in a minute,' West replied. 'Just make sure you're ready to lift off as soon as he's on board.' The pilot gave him the okay signal and West continued, 'Oh, and there's been a slight change of destination …'

*

Glen Lyons sat impatiently in his taxi, while it was delayed in a traffic jam.

'Come on – come on, what's the bloody hold-up?"

'Looks like another friggin' demonstration,' the taxi driver said as he leant out of the window.

Lyons impatiently wound down his window. In the street ahead, there was a noisy clash between two rival groups holding placards and shouting slogans. The police were trying to keep order with little success. A Caucasian group held placards that read, 'No More Asians!' 'Keep Asians Out of Our Jobs!' 'Send 'em Back!' and the predominately Asian group retaliated with, 'Fair Go Aussie!' 'Equal Status for Asians!' and 'We Paid For Our Freedom!'

'Can't you go around?' Lyons yelled at the taxi driver.

'Keep ya shirt on,' the driver replied irritably as he attempted to force his way through the demonstrators and the crowd who had gathered to watch. He inadvertently nudged one of the demonstrators who in turn fell against a couple of rivals and a fight broke out which quickly turned into a melee. One of the pro-Asians was thrown against the side of the cab, his placard filling Lyons' window space: 'War, Communism, Intolerance, What Price Freedom!" Lyons roughly pushed the placard and the demonstrator away as the taxi ploughed its way on through the crowd.

*

While Tan lay in the hospital bed, with a wire frame draped in a sheet covering most of his body and dressing disguising most of his face, Steve stood in the doorway talking to the nurse. She told him that Tan was stable but had been sedated to help him deal with the pain. Steve stood for some time looking despondently at his friend and then returned to the waiting room.

Sally looked up questioningly but Steve shook his head.

'He's as comfortable as can be expected,' he said, mimicking the nurse, and flopping in a chair next to Sally. 'What about Yin Foo? Is he going to arrest us?'

'Probably,' she replied. 'I've asked for a twin share cell.' She smiled brightly, 'There's one bit of good news though, the Navy's picked up the bogus patrol boat and the crew. Yin Foo's gone to the dock to question them.'

'Well, thank God for that. What about the fishing trawler?'

'No news on that yet.' She shook her head. 'They're probably camouflaged and hiding out somewhere in shallow water.'

Dejected, Steve put his head in his hands.

'They'll get them,' Sally said, laying her hand reassuringly across his shoulders.

'But they'll only get the soldiers, not the generals,' he said despondently. 'We need to get the *Luger*, and she's gone. She and the top brass will just move their operation into some other area and start it all over again.'

He'd hardly got the words out of his mouth when he was suddenly hit with an idea. He silently stood and paced, exploring the possibilities in his mind. Arriving at a conclusion, he turned to Sally and said, 'Where did you say Yin Foo had gone?'

'To the Williamstown dock, to interview the crew of the patrol boat, why?'

'And they didn't bring the *Shark* back with them?'

She shook her head. She could tell something was stirring him and her fear started to return. 'Steve?'

'Ah, I've just thought of something I didn't tell Yin Foo. I've got to find him. You stay here in case Tan wakes up. Don't worry, I'll be back as soon as I can … It might take a while.'

'But Steve …'

But Steve wasn't waiting for any argument which he knew she was about to give him. He pecked her on the cheek and strode from the waiting room, leaving her open mouthed and mystified.

Again she called after him but he had already disappeared. She sighed, helplessly.

Chapter 15

Lyons' taxi arrived at the heliport. He paid the driver and got out, taking his luggage with him. He looked towards the helicopter, with its blades whirring, ready for take-off, and waved. He hurried down the path to board but when he was within a few metres of it, the chopper suddenly lifted into the air and flew off. Lyons dropped his luggage, frantically waved his arms, and yelled as he ran forward, but from within the craft his screams could not be heard.

In the passenger seat of the helicopter, West smiled as he turned to his companion Mr. Trench, the Managing Director of Trench International Maritime, whom Jonas had visited only a few days prior.

'That was close,' West said. 'He was early.' The chopper banked and headed out towards the ocean.

*

Steve got out of his taxi and hurried along the wharf. The fake patrol boat was berthed a little way along with several Navy guards standing by on duty. Captain Bryce and his crew were being escorted off the boat by Lieutenant Cooper and a couple of ratings. As Steve approached, Cooper recognised him and waved. 'How's your friend,' he asked.

'Hasn't regained consciousness but he's stable, thanks to you,' Steve replied, smiling.

'When he comes to, tell him we've put this lot out of action. That'll cheer him up.'

'Thanks, and I mean for everything. Where's Yin Foo?' Steve asked as he looked along the wharf for the investigator.

Cooper indicated over his shoulder. 'Just coming ashore.'

Steve nodded and wandered amiably over to Captain Bryce, who was standing nearby with his men, guarded by the shore patrolmen.

'I'm Steve Saunders,' Steve said, 'the guy you tried to ram.'

Without warning, he suddenly hauled off and smashed his fist into Bryce's face. The blood from his shattered nose spattered over Steve's shirt as the corrupt captain groaned and crumpled to the ground.

A couple of guards stepped in to restrain Steve but Cooper intervened, smiling and shaking his head, indicating they were not to interfere. Steve smiled back at him and, with a satisfied smirk, continued along the wharf to join Yin Foo who was just coming down the gang plank.

'Mr Saunders,' the exasperated Yin Foo sighed, 'what are you doing here? I asked you ...'

'The chopper,' Steve interrupted him, 'can we get a loan of the frigate's chopper?'

'What?' Yin Foo exclaimed as if Steve was out of his mind.

*

The sky was overcast with the promise of rain as the *Luger* lay at anchor out beyond the twelve-mile limit. The helicopter, from which West and Trench had just disembarked, banked overhead, returning to the mainland. On the deck, Jonas greeted the new arrivals.

'Thank God you've arrived. It's been like bloody Central Station around here. Choppers and search planes all over the place trying to force us back into Australian waters.' He turned to Brandwell, standing by his side. 'Okay, let's get the tub underway.'

'Which cabin are our friends in?' Trench said as they moved off.

Jonas stopped in mild surprise.

'They're not on board.'

154

Trench and West stopped disbelievingly and turned to him.

'What do you mean? We're not going without them.'

'The *Shark* is not answering our radio calls. We presumed she'd been picked up, or maybe hiding out somewhere, or even scuttled.'

'Keep trying, 'Trench said angrily. 'We're not leaving until we have something definite.'

'But …' Jonas tried to intervene but Trench overrode him,

'They're too important and there's too much money involved. Do you realise what sort of reception we'd get in Bangkok if we arrived without them? We wait.'

Jonas desperately tried to convince him to reassess their situation but Trench was adamant.

Finally, he turned to Brandwell, sighed in resignation, and said, 'Keep signalling the *Shark*.'

Brandwell left reluctantly to obey orders and the others moved off.

*

Sally was still sitting in the waiting room when Robert Heston suddenly appeared. She was so relieved to see a friendly face she hurried to him and impulsively threw her arms around him.

'Oh, Robert, thank you so much for coming.'

He smiled indulgently and patted her shoulder and suggested they take a break and go for a walk. As they wandered down to Fawkner Park, Sally brought Robert up to date on what had been happening. He was horrified that she'd allowed herself to be put in such a dangerous situation but she made light of it saying the important thing was that they'd survived, and quickly changed the subject back to the clinical issues which she knew would distract Robert from further chastising her.

'I think,' she postulated, 'when Steve went out on that last assignment in Vietnam, he was already close to breaking point from the horror, disillusionment, guilt – the whole awful experience. And I believe the burning boy in Vietnam suddenly became a sort of symbol in Steve's mind. I think he saw the boy as the future of the country that was being destroyed and desperately tried to save him from the flames. But Ricketts stopped him and tried to kill Steve, his journalist friend and the boy – a further betrayal.'

'And when Steve survived, that only re-affirmed the guilt in his mind,' Robert nodded, agreeing with her.

'Yes,' she said. 'He needed to save the people and so Tan became the symbol. That's why he feels so strongly, so responsible for Tan and so protective of him.'

'It's ironic that it was Tan who saved Steve in Vietnam,' Robert said.

'And then seeing Tan go up in flames like the boy ...' Sally added.

Robert nodded. 'His failure was coming back to haunt him. But now he has a whole bunch of Vietnamese to save.'

Sally remembered something Steve had said. 'That's why his war is not over. Whatever happens, this time he's got to win. And if he doesn't ...' Her thoughts went unspoken but her fear deepened, not knowing where he was and what he was doing.

'And where is he now?' Robert asked, looking at her steadily and noting her obvious concern.

'I don't know!' she almost shouted in her exasperation. 'He rushed out saying something about forgetting to tell the Commonwealth policeman something that was important and I haven't seen or heard from him since.' She stopped and looked miserably at Robert. 'I'm so frightened for him, Rob.'

He took her arm and led her to a nearby bench and they sat. 'Of course you are, but getting over-emotional is not going to help him – or you. I think you've allowed yourself to get in too deep. It's time to pull back. You've done all you can for him. Now it's up to me to get him back on track. If necessary, I'll just have to pick up the pieces and start again.'

'What do you mean?' She looked at him in utter disbelief. 'Are you suggesting I should just walk out and leave him? He's not just a case history, Robert. It's not whether he needs *me* – I need *him*! I love him!'

Robert looked at her for a long moment and then, almost as if he were talking to a child, he put his arm around her protectively.

'Sally, the doctor doesn't fall in love with the patient, remember? I know it all sounds very romantic, but think about it. Look at the both of you, your backgrounds, your intelligence levels, your potential futures. If he does manage to get well again – and he may never fully recover you know – how long do you think you and he would actually last?'

She carefully removed his arm from her shoulders and turned to him.

'For as long as he'll have me. And if there are pieces to be picked up, I'll pick them up. And the next time, and the next, if necessary.'

He looked at her steadily and slowly realised he had lost her.

'And what about us,' he whispered, the disappointment for a moment breaking through his normal reserve.

Sally sighed. 'There hasn't been an *us* for a long time, Robert,' she said gently. 'Not since just after I met Steve.'

He looked away from her.

'You see, you and I analysed and theorised and intellectualised emotions, but Steve feels them and shows them.' She looked away, not wanting to hurt him any further. 'And he makes me feel them too.'

She remembered something Steve had said to her earlier and she knew exactly what he meant. 'When I'm with him, my guts smile.'

Robert grimaced at this awful expression and finally accepted he was wasting his time. He stood looking down at her despondently.

'Call me if you need me and … good luck.'

He walked off and Sally watched him go.

'Robert,' she called after him. He stopped and turned.

'I'm sorry,' she said simply.

He nodded and continued on his way.

*

In the captain's cabin, a tense Jonas sat talking and drinking a bottle of Scotch with Trench and West. Suddenly the door flew open to reveal an excited Brandwell.

'We've picked up a signal from the *Shark*! She's on her way!'

'And the passengers?' Trench demanded.

'Safe on board,' Brandwell smiled.

'Yes!' exclaimed Jonas, rising to his feet. 'Tell the engine room to fire up. We'll get underway as soon as they're on deck.'

'Wait!' Trench bellowed. 'We'll go in and meet them. It'll save time.'

Brandwell looked anxiously at his captain, 'That'll take us inside the twelve-mile limit.'

'We can't risk it,' Jonas said to Trench.

'For God's sake, look out there,' said West. 'It's night time, the weather's closing in and there's probably not another ship for miles. We'd be in and out again in no time.'

'He's right,' Trench urged, and as a further incentive, 'You want your bonus, take her in.'

Jonas objected to being pressured and it showed on his strained face. There was a tense pause while he decided. Eventually he nodded to Brandwell who hurried from the cabin. Trench and West stood.

'Well, let's go up and welcome them on board,' said Trench, and the three men headed out onto to the deck where a misty rain had begun to cloud the choppy sea. Trench and West stood looking out over the rail while Jonas went to the bridge. The mist, rain and approaching darkness made it impossible to see the *Shark* as the *Luger* sailed back into Australian waters.

Brandwell was monitoring the ship's radar which gave the *Shark's* position.

'Won't be long now,' he informed Jonas as he arrived at his side. 'Only one other ship on the radar now and it looks like she's heading out to sea. You don't think it could be the Navy?'

'I don't think it's the fuckin' Good Ship Lollypop,' said Jonas. 'Keep your eyes open and let me know if she changes course.' He started to leave the bridge saying snidely, 'I'd better go down on deck and join the welcoming committee. Keep a full head of steam. We take only the two passengers on board and send the trawler back.' He turned. 'As soon as we're clear, turn and ram her. I don't want any evidence floating around.'

Brandwell smiled and nodded in agreement as Jonas left the bridge.

He joined Trench and West at the ship's rail saying, as they all squinted into the mist, 'We'll heave-to as soon as we see their signal.'

Brandwell's voice cut through the now howling wind. 'Captain, that other ship on the radar, she's coming around behind us! She's trying to cut us off!'

'Fuck!' Jonas screamed. 'I knew it! Bring her around! Take her back out!'

'Wait!' Trench yelled, pointing, 'There she is! The *Shark*!'

It was true. The *Shark* could now clearly be seen only a short distance away cutting through the mist and rain and rolling heavily.

'There's still time! Bring her about!' Trench yelled.

'No!' screamed Jonas, 'You'll do the lot of us!'

Trench suddenly drew a revolver from his pocket and pointed it directly at Jonas.

'Bring her about, Captain Jonas,' he ordered threateningly. 'I want those men on board.'

Jonas was stunned and furious at having his orders over-ruled and dearly wanted to take the revolver from Trench and shove it up his arse, but he knew time was running out and he had to act quickly.

'How much time have we got before they can intercept us, Brandwell?' he yelled at his Mate.

159

'At their full speed, probably about half an hour,' Brandwell called back. 'They're just on the edge of the screen.'

'Plenty of time,' Trench said.

Against his every instinct Jonas capitulated and yelled to Brandwell angrily, 'Make ready to take on boarders!'

'But Captain …' Brandwell tried to protest.

'Just do it, Mr Brandwell!' Jonas screamed in frustration.

As the *Luger* stopped, some of the crew appeared out of the ships bowels and, with the wind whipping their wet weather gear, they frantically readied the boarding ladder.

The *Shark* came alongside and Hooker stood on the bow with the two Japanese businessmen and five crew members, all dressed in long wet weather gear and rain hats, attempting to hold the *Shark* fast against the *Luger's* hull.

'You've done it again, Hooker!' Jonas called. 'You've got the Australian Navy steamin' right up our arses. Move it! Get the two passengers on board so we can get the hell out of here!'

'No way!' Hooker yelled back. 'We're comin' on board too!'

'Don't be fucking stupid, just the passengers, Hooker!' Jonas ordered.

'No passengers unless you take us too!' was the shouted reply.

Jonas was about to argue further but Trench suddenly cut in, 'For God's sake, let them on board. There's no time to argue!'

'If it wasn't for these incompetent shit-heads, we wouldn't be where we are now!' Jonas snarled back at him.

'They also know the locations of the safe houses,' West reminded him. 'The Immigration authorities would love to get their hands on *that* information. Besides,' he said, with a calculated sneer, 'it's a long way back to Bangkok.'

Jonas reluctantly conceded the point and yelled back to Hooker.

'Okay, you old bastard, get on board. But leave your engine running and jam the steering so it'll take the trawler back in towards the coast. It might fool the Navy into following and it'll give us a bit more time to get back into International waters.'

'Stand by, we're on our way,' Hooker shouted back.

Jonas, Trench and West stood back as the two Japanese, assisted by a couple of the *Shark's* crew, Hooker and the rest, came over the leeward side and onto the deck. The *Shark's* engine was left idling with the trawler tied to the Luger's hull. West and Trench stepped forward, smiling, with hands outstretched to greet their valuable guests.

'Terribly sorry for the inconvenience, gentlemen ...'

But the moment was frozen mid-sentence by the loud sound of four automatic weapons being cocked. Startled, Trench, West and Jonas swung around to be confronted by the *Shark's* 'crew': Yin Foo, Lieutenant Cooper, two naval men and Steve. All except Steve were armed with automatic weapons which they had concealed under their long, wet weather coats.

'What the hell!' Jonas exclaimed in surprise. 'Who the fuck are you?'

'Detective Sergeant Yin Foo,' the Chinese man answered, 'Australian Commonwealth police, and these other gentlemen are from the HMAS *Yarra* which will be joining us in just a few minutes.'

Steve stepped forward and said, 'And I'm Steve Saunders, a friend of Nguyen Tan, who you tried to kill along with his father and mother. I don't think we've met.'

Jonas spun around to glare at Hooker who was looking very guilty.

'They were waiting for us off the coast. They followed your Jap friends,' he said contritely.

The Japanese were looking very uneasy.

From a hidden vantage point and unseen by the group, Brandwell was sizing up the situation. He also now carried an automatic weapon and crouched low, watching while Yin Foo informed Jonas and the others how the Japanese businessmen and the money had led them to the *Luger*.

'We're in International waters – you have no jurisdiction,' protested the irate Jonas.

'Statistically not quite in International waters, I'm afraid,' replied Cooper, 'and frankly, even if you were we wouldn't give a damn.'

'This is piracy!' an outraged Trench roared.

'Well, that's the pot calling the kettle black, Mr Trench,' Cooper replied sarcastically.

Also armed and unseen, Ricketts crept up to Brandwell and crouched beside him.

'You can bet your life they've got back-up on the way,' Ricketts whispered.

'But how far away?' Brandwell whispered back. 'There might still be a chance. Get onto the engine room. Tell 'em full speed ahead.' He tapped his gun. 'You and me will keep this lot occupied until we're in the clear. Once we scatter them, the crew will be able to help out. We'll even have a few important hostages.'

'Right,' Ricketts said as he moved off, 'you take 'em from the port side and I'll take them from the lee. We'll have 'em in a cross-fire.'

Brandwell nodded and they moved off in opposite directions. Ricketts scuttled down to the engine room but did not relate the message for full steam ahead as Brandwell had ordered. Instead, he burst in screaming to the two engineers. 'Alright, Chief, the shit's hit the fan! Both of you get the hell up on deck and help out!' He grabbed an axe from the bulkhead and moved to the fuel intake line.

'What the fuck are you doing, Ricketts?' the chief yelled back in alarmed astonishment.

'The captain ordered us to scuttle! We're gunna abandon ship! Now get out! Move it! Move it!' he screamed.

Panicked by his urgency and with no time to think, the chief and his mate didn't stop to argue. They fled from the engine room, grabbing a couple of heavy tools for weapons as they went. Ricketts raised the axe and smashed it into the fuel intake line, sending diesel spurting like a black fountain. He struck again and again, each time rupturing the line and causing yet more jets of fuel to spurt and cascade. He grabbed an oil rag from a bench, quickly took a cigarette lighter from his pocket, ignited the oil-soaked cloth and, standing back, threw it into the fuel that was already pooling on the engine room deck and spreading. The fuel ignited with a 'pop' and quickly spread, flames shooting up and out, soon devouring everything in their path. Satisfied with his work, Ricketts grabbed his AK47 and ran from the engine room. He knew they didn't have a chance and hoped the fire and gunfire would distract the boarders long enough for him to get over the side onto the unattended *Shark* and escape. Leaving the burning engine room, he went straight to a vantage point on the leeward side near the ladder down to the *Shark* and waited for his opportunity. After a moment he signalled Brandwell that he was ready.

Brandwell jumped from his hiding place and opened fire on Steve and the others. The gunfire spurted across the deck, wounding one of the naval ensigns and scattering the rest of the group who all dived for cover and returned the fire. Ricketts fired a burst and then dived for the rail and the ladder down to the *Shark*. Steve found himself unarmed and once again under fire for the second time since Vietnam. He scrunched himself in a ball behind a crate lying on the deck, his face showing the tension, strain and fear. Several other shots began to ring out from the *Luger's* crew who had dived for weapons.

'Lay down your arms!' Yin Foo yelled. 'We've got your captain, and the Navy is on its way!'

There was another burst of fire in answer and Cooper grabbed hold of Jonas.

'Captain Jonas, order them to cease firing! Immediately!'

'You order 'em!' Jonas replied.

The gunfire continued and Brandwell yelled, unaware that Ricketts was deserting the ship, 'Your side, Ricketts! Let's take 'em out!'

Brandwell stood for a clearer shot expecting back-up from Ricketts and a burst of fire from Cooper hit him squarely in the chest, ripping it open, blood spurting as he was violently flung back by the force of the bullets. He dropped to the deck, writhed in jerking spasms of agony as the shots tore the life from his body, and went still.

At that moment smoke and flames began belching from the companionway.

'Jesus, we're on fire!' Jonas roared.

The alarm soon spread, everyone turning to watch the flames that were belching from the engine room and leaving everyone in a quandary as to what to do next, continue the battle or put out the fire.

'Lay down your arms and get that bloody fire out,' Cooper yelled, 'or we're all done for!' The gunfire finally and sporadically faded and stopped as men ran for hoses to fight the growing inferno.

Suddenly Steve caught a glimpse of Ricketts, silhouetted by the light of the flames, as he mounted the rail and went over the side. Oblivious to the danger and all fear suddenly gone, he screamed Ricketts' name and desperately scrambled after him. It took time for Ricketts to get down the ladder, being hampered by his weapon and the swaying of the ladder from the waves pounding the *Shark*. Steve reached the rail while Ricketts was only halfway down. He clambered over and down the ladder after him, eventually letting go and flinging himself at Ricketts, landing on the fleeing man's back, causing them both to fall and slam onto the heaving deck below. Ricketts' AK47 tore loose and skidded across the deck. The two men hit the deck hard and rolled immediately, struggling for supremacy, with Ricketts finishing up on top of Steve who struggled violently to free himself. Ricketts smashed him in the face and raised his arm for another blow but Steve was ready for it this time and twisted. The blow glanced off his cheek and at the same time he brought his knee up viciously into his opponent's groin. Ricketts grunted from the excruciating pain but hung on to Steve's neck, attempting to get a stranglehold. Steve grabbed his shoulders and pulled him forward, head-butting his opponent and opening a gash on his forehead, which caused Ricketts to loosen his grip enough for Steve to free himself from the vice-like hold. He heaved the ex-sergeant's body from him and scrambled to his feet just as Ricketts regained his footing and dived for the gun.

Steve flew at him throwing heavy punches at his head and body. The blows made Ricketts groggy as he staggered back towards the wheelhouse, his hand coming in contact with a large, heavy spanner. He grabbed it and swung it at Steve in a vicious swipe but Steve ducked and the spanner sailed past his head, missing him by millimetres. The next blow Steve blocked with his left forearm and swung his right fist hard into Ricketts' temple. The blow clouded Ricketts' vision and he dropped the spanner which clattered to the deck. Steve took the advantage and moved in, beating his enemy mercilessly with heavy blows to the head and body. Finally, he grabbed his adversary by the shoulders and swung his head into the wheelhouse wall. The crack of skull on steel could be heard above the *Shark's* idling motor and crashing sea water. The deck heaved again from the impact of the waves and Ricketts staggered and fell. Steve grabbed the AK47 that Ricketts had dropped and released the safety catch. His face twisted in hate and revenge, he pointed the gun at Ricketts and pulled the trigger.

The rounds bit into the deck near Ricketts' head, splinters of wood exploding into the air. Ricketts attempted to shield himself and lay squirming, trying to escape the deadly explosions that erupted around him. The burst of fire stopped and Steve stood over his hated foe, the rifle levelled at his head.

Suddenly there was comparative silence. The gunfire from the *Luger* had ceased but voices shouting instructions could be heard from the deck above. Ricketts looked up at the man he had failed to kill so many times, expecting at any moment to feel the searing pain of hot lead tearing into his flesh.

'I should've made sure of you in 'Nam,' he snarled.

'I guess you should have, Sergeant Arse-hole,' Steve replied.

Suddenly, the harsh glare from the naval frigate's searchlight illuminated the scene.

Chapter 16

A contingent from the *Yarra* boarded and with the help of water hoses and fire fighting equipment from the frigate, the fire was eventually brought under control, leaving the *Luger* a smouldering wreck. Jonas, the Japanese businessmen, Ricketts and the crew were handcuffed, shackled together and transferred to the *Yarra* for the return trip to Williamstown. A suddenly obsequious Hooker was now only too eager to turn against the organisation and give evidence now that all was lost and he and his crew were also arrested and transported to the *Yarra*. The *Shark*, crewed by a couple of Royal Australian Naval men, would follow the frigate back to port. Exhausted, Steve sat on the deck with his head between his knees.

Yin Foo appeared at his side and smiled down at the man who had risked his life and sanity in his determination to bring the people smugglers to justice.

'If you're ready to go now, Mr Saunders, I think there's a worried young lady waiting for you. And don't worry, I think we'll be able to handle it from here on in – unless, of course, you're also a lawyer and intend acting as Prosecutor at the trial,' he added sardonically.

He held out a plastic evidence bag filled with the contents of Jonas's safe.

'I found a few good pieces of evidence in the safe in Jonas's cabin that the fire didn't get to. Worth a pretty penny, I should say – bribes, Hooker tells me. He's full of helpful information,' he smiled.

Steve looked up at him ruefully.

'Just give me a call if I can help you out anymore – but I warn you I don't do washing and ironing.'

Yin Foo chuckled. 'I'll tell my brother-in-law; he'll be very disappointed.'

'You know, I was very suspicious of you when we first met,' Steve said, eyeing the man above him. 'I mean, who'd believe a Chinaman called *Yin Foo* claiming to be a Commonwealth policeman was the genuine article?'

Yin Foo laughed. 'I'll change my name to Kojak if you think that would help – or maybe Charlie Chan.'

'What's going to happen now?' Steve asked, smiling and changing the subject. 'With the refugees and the rest of the gang, I mean?'

'Oh, we'll eventually track them down,' Yin Foo sighed confidently. 'Hooker knows the whereabouts of the safe houses and we'll soon get the locations of the farms, factories and sweatshops the illegals are sent to.'

'But the refugees – what will happen to them?'

Yin Foo shrugged. 'Detention camps – they'll be processed eventually. Some might be able to stay.'

'And the others – the sick, the old, the weak and dispossessed?'

Another shrug from the policeman. 'If they don't meet our criteria, they'll be sent back.'

Steve scowled. 'And the meek will inherit the earth and the innocent will be spared,' he said cynically. 'It's such a compassionate world.'

Yin Foo smiled benignly, giving his impression of an inscrutable old Chinaman. 'Confucius say, "Compassion is something to aim for. But in the meantime, carry a big stick." '

Steve smiled. 'I think you made that one up.'

Yin Foo grinned.

Chapter 17

Tan lay in the hospital bed, conscious but still sedated against the worst of the pain. Nodding in tiredness, Sally sat by his side. Tan glanced at the door as it opened and Steve burst in.

'The war's over and us goodies won,' he announced, smiling broadly.

At the sound of his voice, Sally's eyes sprang open and she turned and stared at him in utter relief and happiness, ran to him and threw her arms around him.

'Oh, Steve,' she cried. 'Thank God!'

He held her close, kissing her head, the closeness and comforting smell of her rejuvenating him.

He released her and moved to Tan's bedside, looking down at him.

'How are you, son?' Steve smiled.

'Much better now,' Tan managed to reply through the dressing on his face, which concealed his relieved expression. 'How are *you*?'

'Fine, just fine,' he replied, his arm around Sally.

'What happened to you this time?' she asked wryly, noticing the dressings on the cuts and bruises on his fists and face and desperate for the information.

'Later,' he said. 'The baddies are all caught and pretty soon there'll be raids going on all over the place, closing down all the safe houses, the sweat shops and the drug factories. The whole operation will be kaput.'

Sally smiled and hugged him again. Tan breathed a sigh of contentment but soon another emotion took over and his eyes clouded with sadness.

'Steve,' he mumbled through the dressing, 'on behalf of my mother, my father, and myself, I thank you most sincerely … Our family has been avenged … and I am hardly worthy of it.'

'What are you talking about, mate? You've played a big part in rounding up these guys.' Steve smiled.

'You put yourself in great danger for us,' Tan said softly and with great difficulty he continued. 'There is something I now have to tell you.'

Steve and Sally frowned in concern for their friend who was obviously having great difficulty with his next statement. Steve went to lay his hand on Tan's shoulder, but seeing him in such a painful condition, he quickly had second thoughts.

'Forget it, Tan,' he said instead. 'There's going to be plenty of …'

But Tan cut him off.

'No, you must know.'

There was an awkward pause before he could bring himself to continue while Sally and Steve looked at each other questioningly. Tan took the largest breath his injuries would allow and began haltingly.

'Back in Vietnam … when we first met … It was not I who saved you … It was the Vietcong.'

Sally and Steve could not comprehend or believe what they were hearing.

'What?' Steve said quietly, still unable to understand.

Tan continued slowly.

'They found you and dressed your wounds and brought you back to my village … They put you in the cart and ordered me to take you back to the Australian lines.' He continued haltingly. 'I was to infiltrate the base and spy for them … They said the Australians would treat me like a hero … because I was just a young kid, no one would suspect me … They didn't … You see …' he swallowed painfully, 'I was a runner for the VC … I believed I was doing my bit to free our country.' There was a long embarrassed pause. 'My family did not know.'

Steve was completely lost for words as the truth was finally revealed. He and Sally could only stare in disbelief at the revelation.

'But ... Why did you come to Australia? Why did you come back to Steve?' Sally asked, incredulously. 'The North Vietnamese won.'

'It was very difficult,' Tan explained. 'You see ... my parents were capitalists. After the war, they were sent into the country to be "re-educated". I had betrayed my family ... I was deeply ashamed ... They would have found out that I had brought them dishonour ... I had to escape ...' His eyes shifted to Steve. 'You'd given me your address in Australia...'

He trailed off and there was a long, emotional silence as the two men looked at each other. Tears began to well up in Tan's eyes. It was obvious that their deep feelings for all they had shared were more than could be put into words.

Eventually, Steve took a step closer to Tan and stood looking down at him. Finally he said softly, 'You'd better get well soon. I'm gunna need you at the garage.'

Steve turned and headed for the door. Sally could do nothing but watch him go.

'But ...' Tan said, stopping Steve from leaving, 'I betrayed you – I used you.'

Steve stopped for a long beat and slowly turned back.

'I guess we both sort of used each other,' he said, looking at Tan with a new-found understanding. He shrugged. 'Good friends do that.'

Steve turned and left the room. Sally smiled at Tan, gently patted his hand and followed. A pretty Vietnamese nurse entered as Sally was leaving.

'Look after him,' Sally smiled at the nurse. 'We want him back real soon.'

The nurse returned her smile, nodded and moved to tidy Tan's bed. His eyes smiled at Sally as she left and gradually his attention was drawn to the pretty nurse. He appraised her shyly but admiringly.

Arm in arm, Steve and Sally walked from the hospital entrance. There was a contented silence that hung between them as it does with people in love. Finally, Sally looked at him and said, 'So, you won your war. How do you feel?'

Steve thought about his reply for a long moment before he said, 'Justified. I was scared shitless of course, – but the main thing is, I coped without losing it.' There was another pause. 'I guess there's always going to be a danger of a remission and I just have to learn to live with it. I can never forget what happened over there in 'Nam, it's something that's now a part of me. But I think I'm getting it more into perspective and learning to deal with it. I don't think there's really an absolute cure but as long as I can go on coping and dealing with it, maybe I'll manage. We'll see.'

They walked on for a few more moments and then, without looking at her, he said, conversationally, 'So, I guess you can wrap up your thesis now.'

Sally stopped and turned to him in surprise.

'You knew?' He remained silent. 'How long?'

He stopped and turned back to face her with a smile.

'A while. You shouldn't have left it lying around on your computer for the patient to see.'

She searched his eyes for a sign of what he was thinking but the mystery remained. She dropped her eyes from his and said awkwardly, 'When I started … I didn't realise I was going to … fall in love with you. I'm sorry,' she said simply but honestly. 'That must've been awful for you. Do you mind – about the thesis, I mean?'

He shrugged and smiled. 'Like I said, people use each other all the time in all sorts of ways … especially lovers.'

He linked her arm through his and they continued to walk away. 'Anyway,' she said, 'I've changed my mind. I've decided not to go ahead with it.'

'Why not,' he replied, 'it might make a good story.'

They moved out onto the street and into the growing dawn.

As they drove to the garage Steve saw that Splicer had arrived and opened up.

Looking into the workshop, Steve said, 'Where's Su- Su?'

'I sold the bitch,' Splicer replied. 'Some fool of a young guy who's a maniac mechanic made me an offer I couldn't refuse; poor sucker. You stayin' on for the day?' he asked, waving and acknowledging Sally sitting in the front of Steve's car.

'No,' Steve replied, 'I'm just picking up something I need. You okay to stay on?'

'As long as you like,' Splicer answered happily.

'Thanks,' said Steve. 'Oh, by the way, someone will probably be delivering my boat back today sometime.'

'You catch anything?' Splicer asked.

'You could say that,' Steve replied enigmatically.

On the outskirts of the city, Steve's car pulled up at the weather-worn and ageing local war memorial and they both got out. The lone stone soldier, head bent, his hands resting on the reversed rifle, seemed to look down at them as if acknowledging their respect.

They crossed to the shrine and stood looking at it for a while before Steve took a screwdriver and thin paintbrush from his pocket and opened the can of black paint he'd picked up at the garage. He stepped over the cast iron railing and dipped the small brush into the paint.

Under the inscription that read, "At the going down of the sun and in the morning, we shall remember them", he carefully painted, "And all of those who managed to survive."

Epilogue

The older Steve and Tan drove away from the memorial and headed for home.

Home for Steve was now a comfortable, renovated, four-bedroom suburban house on the outskirts of Williamstown in Victoria. There was a well-kept lawn and front garden, landscaped in a mixture of old-fashioned and modern styles, with flowering camellias and rhododendrons and a shrub-bordered path.

As they pulled up outside, they were greeted by a rowdy group of guests. Joey and Finch were there with their wives; Splicer had his latest 'girlfriend', a rather strong-minded, grey-haired woman in her late fifties who adored him. There were also three Vietnamese, two young women and a young man, standing with their Australian partners and two young Eurasian toddlers waving and laughing in greeting.

'Hi, Dad! You're late,' the adopted Vietnamese, Stephen Junior, Nancy and Sarah called out to Steve. 'Mum's got it in for you,' they chorused.

He waved back as he got out of the car and Tan hurried around to help him.

'I'm alright, you bloody old fusspot,' Steve hissed softly as Tan held out his walking stick. 'I'm not a fucking old cripple, you know.'

Tan grinned. 'Yes you are.'

Through the front door came the attractive Vietnamese nurse who had looked after Tan in the hospital all those years ago and ended up marrying him. Now middle-aged and wearing a striking pink apron, she waved at Tan who grinned and waved back. Sally followed her out, holding a baby in her arms. Steve paused to admire his now grey-haired, elderly wife and smiled. She's still a remarkably beautiful woman, he thought, as he walked up the path toward her.

'You're late,' she chided him. 'Your new grandson is just about to go down for his sleep. I've made the salad, the barbecue is on and everything's ready for you to start cooking.'

Ah, life's so good, Steve thought, as he kissed Sally on the cheek, laid the walking stick aside, took the baby from her and held him in his arms.

The End

Bryon Williams, ex-stage and television actor, script writer, producer, director turned novelist, has now retired to a Retirement Village in Brisbane. Two of his previous novels, *The Grumpy Old Withered of Oz*, a comedic, semi-autobiographical book about the frustrations of ageing and life as his wife's carer in the not-so-fast lane of the *Zzzzzzzzz* Generation, and *The Twilight Escort Agency*, an hilarious and bawdy account of a mythical escort agency for the 'more mature' client, have enjoyed very positive independent reader response, as has his third novel, the whimsical comedy crime-fantasy, ideal for cat lovers, *Code Name: Millicent – The Cat Intelligence Agent Who Came Out of the Cold*.

Tourist from the Light, an intriguing paranormal romance with an underlying theme of a thought-provoking alternative spiritual philosophy, followed. This novel, *The Burning Boy*, is his fifth publication.

Bryon's beloved wife of 45 years, Marie, suffered a disastrous stroke in 2000 and he retired to become her full-time carer until she passed on in 2014. Bryon went on to write a memoir of his career and his married life, *A Light at the End*, which received numerous 5-star favourable reviews.

With the legalisation of gay marriage and acceptance of sexual equality, Bryon then changed course and wrote *Naked Warrior*, a gay, erotic love story based on Bryon's belief in Reincarnation.

Intrigued and inspired by an old friend's unresolved story of the tragic murder of her daughter in 1988, they collaborated to co-write *Not in the Public Interest*, published in 2019.